John Frost

Old Hickory

Young Folks' Life of Gen. Andrew Jackson

John Frost

Old Hickory
Young Folks' Life of Gen. Andrew Jackson

ISBN/EAN: 9783744783736

Printed in Europe, USA, Canada, Australia, Japan

Cover: Foto ©Raphael Reischuk / pixelio.de

More available books at **www.hansebooks.com**

OLD ROUGH AND READY SERIES

OLD HICKORY

YOUNG FOLKS' LIFE

OF

GEN. ANDREW JACKSON

SEVENTH PRESIDENT OF THE UNITED STATES

By JOHN FROST

ILLUSTRATED

BOSTON
LEE AND SHEPARD PUBLISHERS
NEW YORK
CHARLES T. DILLINGHAM
1887

PREFACE.

N the 8th day of June, less than one month ago—died, in the fullness of his years and honours, the great citizen and soldier, ANDREW JACKSON,

It will be for the men of another age to pass a calm and enduring judgment upon the influence of his remarkable career upon the character and destinies of the nation. But as a military commander of the most splendid abilities; as a statesman who has occupied the highest place in the gift of the people, with a courage and strength of intellect which have made his name familiar through the world; as a brave, patriotic and high-souled AMERICAN; he is even now contemplated by the men of every opinion and party.

(3)

He lived a hero, and died a Christian. He is gone from a world where he was recognised as among the greatest of men, to an immortal companionship with the greatest and purest of all the ages.

We have, in this little volume, sketched his history with carefulness and candour, and present the record to our young countrymen, to be placed with that of the life of our Washington, among the models to be imitated by all who would attain a similar elevation in the world.

CONTENTS.

CHAPTER I.

CHAPTER II.

CHAPTER III.

CHAPTER IV.

CHAPTER V.

CHAPTER VI.

CHAPTER VII.

CHAPTER VIII.

CHAPTER IX.

CHAPTER X.

CHAPTER XI.

CHAPTER XII.

CHAPTER XIII.

CHAPTER XXII.

CHAPTER XXIII

CHAPTER XXIV.

CHAPTER XXV.

CHAPTER XXVI.

CHAPTER XXVII.

LIFE

OF

ANDREW JACKSON.

CHAPTER I.

HIS BIRTH AND PARENTAGE.

ANDREW JACKSON was born on the 15th of March, 1767, in the state of South Carolina. This distinguished hero can trace no line of splendid ancestry. He may, however, boast of having sprung from a race distinguished for honesty, courage, and generous hospitality.

His father (Andrew) was the youngest son of a Scotch family, whose ancestors had at some remote period emigrated to the north of Ireland. To escape the troubles brought upon that country by the English government, Andrew Jackson, with his wife and two sons, Hugh and Robert, emigrated to Charleston, South Carolina, in 1765. Having

purchased a tract of land in what was then called
the "Waxhaw settlement," (about forty-five miles
above Camden, and near the boundary line of North
Carolina,) he left Charleston shortly after, and settled here with his family. In two years after his
arrival at the Waxhaw settlement, Andrew Jackson,
the subject of our biography, was born. Thus do
we see that to no long line of titled ancestors, to no
extensive connection with the wealthy and influential, is General Jackson indebted for the high place
he occupies in the confidence and affections of his
countrymen, and the rank he is destined to hold
among the good and the great of mankind.

The progress of General Jackson, from the
" plough to the presidency," is an instructive and
encouraging lesson to the youth of his country.

Shortly after the birth of Jackson, his father died,
leaving himself and his two brothers under the sole
protection and guardianship of their mother. And
well did this remarkable woman deserve and execute
the duties of her station. It has been said, that
many great men have been indebted for their success
to the early principles and lessons inculcated by a
wise mother. The life of General Jackson is an
additional proof of the correctness of this remark;
for the many acts of female heroism, and devotion

both to her family and her adopted country, prove
that the mother of our hero was a woman of no
common mind. She appears to have been an exemplary woman, and to have executed the arduous
duties which had devolved on her with great faith-
fulness and with much success. To the lessons she
inculcated on the youthful minds of her sons was,
no doubt, owing, in a great measure, that fixed opposition to British tyranny and oppression which
afterward so much distinguished them. Often
would she spend the winter's evenings in recount-
ing to them the sufferings of their grandfather at
the siege of Carrickfergus, and the oppressions
exercised by the nobility of Ireland over the labour
ing poor; impressing it upon them, as a first duty,
to expend their lives, if it should become necessary,
in defending and supporting the natural rights of
man.

Inheriting but a small patrimony from their father,
it was impossible that all the sons could receive an
expensive education. The two eldest were, therefore, only taught the rudiments of their mother
tongue, at a common country school. But Andrew,
being intended by his mother for the ministry, was
sent to a flourishing academy at the Waxhaw
meeting-house, superintended by Mr. Humphries

Here he was placed on the study of the dead lan
guages, and continued until the revolutionary war,
extending its ravages into that section of South
Carolina where he then was, rendered it necessary
.hat every one should betake himself to the American standard, seek protection with the enemy, or
flee his country.

CHAPTER II.

LIFE DURING THE REVOLUTIONARY WAR.

N 1775, when the revolutionary war broke out, Andrew Jackson was but eight years old. Although it was some years afterwards when its bloody footsteps approached his residence, he heard of its battles and its horrors from afar, and may be said to have grown up amidst war's alarms. All around him the men were training themselves for battle, and from his mother and teacher he received constant lessons of patriotic devotion.

It was not long, however, before Jackson had an opportunity of being an eye-witness to the butcheries of a savage war. South Carolina was invaded by the British in 1779, and in the early part of 1780 the war was pushed with renewed vigour, and reached the hitherto peaceful settlement of the Waxhaws.

On the 29th May, 1780, a division of the American army, under Colonel Buford, was attacked in the Waxhaw settlement by Colonel Tarleton, and suffered a total defeat. One hundred and fifteen of the Americans were killed, and one hundred and fifty desperately wounded. Some of the men had received no less than thirteen wounds. The Waxhaw meeting-house was converted into a hospital; and here had the young Jackson an opportunity of witnessing the horrors of war. The mangled bodies of his countrymen, presented a sad confirmation of those impressions made upon his youthful mind by the tales of English cruelty which he had so often heard from his mother and kindred.

Shortly after this, Mrs. Jackson, with her two sons, Robert and Andrew (she had already lost her eldest, Hugh, who perished in the battle of Stono), retired before the invading army into North Carolina. Here she remained but a short time, and, returning to the Waxhaws, her two sons entered the ranks of the American army, and were present at the battle of Hanging Rock, on the 6th of August, 1780, in which their corps particularly distinguished itself. This was General Jackson's first field, and he was little over thirteen years old on the day of the battle.

In the month of September following, Mrs. Jack son and her sons, with most of the Waxhaw settlers, were again compelled to retire before the British army into North Carolina. They returned, however, in February, 1781, as soon as they heard that Lord Cornwallis had crossed the Yadkin. The war had now assumed a degree of savage ferocity. Private revenge, on both sides, found ready means of gratification in this system of partisan warfare. The laws were not enforced, and there were no courts to protect innocence or punish crime,—men hunted each other like beasts of prey, and the savages were outdone in cruelty. In such a school was our hero tutored. Boys, big enough to carry muskets, incurred the dangers of men. Robert and Andrew Jackson had their guns and their horses, and were almost always in company with some armed party of their kindred and neighbours. Men could not sleep unguarded in their own houses, without danger of being surprised and murdered.

It was upon such an occasion, that Andrew Jackson gave the first illustration of that quickness of conception, and readiness of action, which afterwards placed him in the highest rank of military chieftains. A patriot captain, named Lands, desired to spend a night with his family. The two

Jacksons and six others constituted his guard; they were in all nine men and seven muskets. Having no expectations of an attack, they all, with the exception of a British deserter, who was one of the party, went to sleep. Lands' house was in the centre of an enclosed yard, and had two doors, facing east and west. In front of the east door stood a forked apple-tree. In the south-west corner of the yard were a corn-crib and stable, under one roof, ranging east and west. On the south was a wood, and through this wood passed the road which led to the house.

A party of the Tories had become apprised of Lands' return, and had determined to surprise and kill him.

Approaching through the wood, and tying their horses behind the stable, they divided into two parties, one going round the east end of the stable, intending to enter the east door of the house, while the other went round the west end, making for the west door. At this moment, the soldier, who was awake, hearing some noise in the direction of the stable, went out to see what was the matter, and perceived the party, which was entering the yard at the east end of the building. Running back in terror, he seized Andrew Jackson, who was nearest

JACKSON'S PRESENCE OF MIND.

the door, by the hair, exclaiming, "the Tories are upon us!" Our young hero ran out, and putting nis gun through the fork of the apple-tree, hailed the approaching band. Having repeated his hail and received no answer, and perceiving that the party still rapidly advanced, and were now only a few rods distant, he fired. A volley was returned, which killed the soldier, who, having aroused the inmates of the house, had followed young Jackson, and was standing near him. The other band of Tories had now emerged from the west end of the stable, and mistaking the discharge of the advance party, then nearly on a line between them and the apple-tree, for the fire of a sallying party from the house, commenced a sharp fire upon their own friends. Thus both parties were brought to a stand. Young Andrew, after discharging his gun, returned into the house; and with two others commenced a fire from the west door, where both of his companions were shot down, one of them with a mortal wound.

The Tories still kept up the fire upon each other, as well as upon the house, until startled by the sound of a cavalry bugle in the distance,—they be-took themselves to their horses, and fled. The charge was sounded by a Major Isbel, of the neighbourhood, who had not a man with him, but, hearing the firing, and knowing that Lands was attacked, gave the blast upon his trumpet to alarm the assailants.

General Jackson was then only fourteen years old; but who does not recognise in the boy of 1781 the general of 1814? By his fire from the apple-tree he brought the enemy to a stand, and saved his little party from capture and massacre; by rushing down upon the enemy on the night of December 1814, he saved an army from capture, and a city from plunder.

It was not long after the above occurrence tha about forty of the Waxhaw settlers, among whom were young Jackson, had rendezvoused at the meeting-house. After their return from North Carolina, the British commander had despatched Major Coffin, with a corps of light dragoons, to the settlement. When the enemy approached the place of rendezvous, they kept a band of Tories, dressed in the common garb of the country, in front, so that the patriots who had been in expectation of a friendly company, under Captain Nisbett, were completely deceived, and fell an easy prey to this stratagem. Eleven of them were taken prisoners, the rest with difficulty fled, scattering, and betaking themselves

to the woods for concealment. Of those who thus
escaped, though closely pursued, were Andrew Jackson and his brother, who, entering a secret bend in
a creek that was close at hand, obtained a momentary respite from danger, and avoided, for the night,
the pursuit of the enemy. The next day, however,
having gone to a neighbouring house for the purpose of procuring something to eat, they were
broken in upon, and made prisoners, by Coffin's dragoons and a party of Tories who accompanied
them. The young men, with a view to security,
had placed their horses in the wood, on the margin
of a small creek, and posted on the road which led
by the house a sentinel, that they might have information of any approach, and in time to be able
to elude it. But the Tories, who were well acquainted with the country and the passes through
the forest, had unfortunately passed the creek at the
very point where the horses and baggage of oui
young soldiers were deposited, and taken possession
of them. Having done this, they approached cau-
tiously the house, and were almost at the door before they were discovered. To escape was impossible, and both were made prisoners. Being placed
under guard, Andrew was ordered, in a very impe-
rious tone, by a British officer, to clean his boots,

which had become muddied in crossing the creek. This order he positively and peremptorily refused to obey; alleging that he looked for such treatment as a prisoner of war had a right to expect. Incensed at his refusal, the officer aimed a blow at his head with a drawn sword, which would very probably have terminated his existence had he not parried its effects by throwing up his left hand, on which he received a severe wound, the mark of which he bore until his death. His brother, at the same time, for a similar offence, received a deep cut on the head, which subsequently occasioned his death. They were both now taken to jail, where, separated and confined, they were treated with marked severity, until a few days after the battle before Camden, when, in consequence of a partial exchange, effected by the intercessions and exertions of their mother, and Captain Walker of the militia, they were both released from confinement.

An anecdote may here be related, illustrative of young Jackson's energy of character. During his confinement at Camden, General Greene made his unsuccessful attack on the British forces stationed there under Lord Rawdon. Camden is situated on a hill. Greene had encamped on Hobkirk's Hill, about a mile distant, and in full view of the redoubt in which the prisoners were confined.

By the signs and sounds around him, on the 24th of April, young Jackson became satisfied that the British intended to surprise the American army, which, under no apprehension of an attack, rested in perfect security. Jackson felt convinced that this would be attempted on the morning of the 25th, and he was most anxious to witness the conflict. This, however, was forbidden by the intervention of a thick plank fence, that ran around the redoubt, and completely shut out the view of the surrounding country. The board fence was thoroughly examined, but not a hole or crevice was to be found through which his eager eye could obtain a view of Greene's encampment. As a last resource, he set to work with an old razor-blade, which had been furnished the prisoners to eat their rations with, and working during most of the night, he continued to dig one of the knots out of the pine planks, with which the fence was constructed, and through this he obtained a full view of Greene's encampment.

During the next day, however, he was doomed to witness the defeat of the American army, with the reflection that his imprisonment was not only to be protracted, but to be shared with new victims to British cruelty.

CHAPTER III.

HORTLY after their release, Andrew Jackson lost his only brother, who died from the effects of the wound received at the hands of the brutal officer, as related in the preceding chapter. To add to his afflictions, his mother, worn down by grief, and her incessant exertions to provide clothing and other comforts for the suffering prisoners who had been taken from her neighbourhood, expired in a few weeks after her son, near the lines of the enemy, in the vicinity of Charleston. He—the last and only surviving child, confined to a bed of sickness, occasioned by the sufferings he had been compelled to undergo while a prisoner, and by getting wet on his return from captivity—was thus left in the wide world without a human being with whom he could claim near relationship. The small-pox, about the same time, hav ing made its appearance upon him, had well-nigh terminated his sorrows and his existence.

Recovering, however, from his complicated afflictions, he entered upon the enjoyment of his estate, which, though small, would have been sufficient to have given him a liberal education. Circumstances, however, led to his expending this patrimonial property with too profuse a hand. During the occupation of Charleston by the British, a number of the polished inhabitants of that city had retired to the Waxhaw settlement, and there remained. With some of these young men Jackson had contracted habits of intimacy, and at the evacuation of Charleston he accompanied them in their return to the city Not wishing to be behind his companions in expenditure, his small property soon melted away, and he was left with only a fine mare, which he had carried along with him from the Waxhaw settlement. She too was at length staked against a sum of money in a game of "rattle and snap." Jackson won the game, and, taking a sudden resolution, he put the money in his pocket, paid his bill, and bidding adieu to his friends, he started for the Waxhaws. Here, having collected the little remains of his property, he took leave of the friends of his youth, and starting for Salisbury, N. C., he placed himself in the

office of Spruce M'Cay, Esq., then an eminent coun-
sellor there, with the view of preparing himself
for the practice of law. This was in the winter
of 1784.

Thus did young Jackson, with an effort of his
inborn energy, cut short his career of dissipation—
and his reformation was thorough and enduring.
He afterwards continued his studies under Colonel
Stokes, also an eminent lawyer, and in a little more
than two years received a license to practise law.
As an evidence of the estimation in which he was
at that time held by the influential men of North
Carolina, he soon after received from the governor
the appointment of Solicitor for the western district
of that state—embracing the present state of **Tennessee.**

CHAPTER IV.

GENERAL JACKSON'S EMIGRATION TO TENNESSEE.—ANECDOTES OF HIS LIFE WHILE PRACTISING AS A LAWYER.

N the year 1788, accompanied by Judge M'Nairy, General Jackson, then twenty-one years old, crossed the mountains, for the purpose of discharging the duties imposed upon him by his recent appointment, and seeking employment in his profession. He took up his residence for some time at Jonesborough, then the principal seat of Justice in the Western District. In the year 1789, he visited the settlements on the Cumberland River. On account of the frequent and terrible forays made by the Choctaw and Cherokee Indians from the South, most of the settlers at this time were living in stations, and but few separate cabins were to be found; and it was some time before these were scattered over the country. During this time, Jackson made frequent professional visits from

Jonesborough to the settlements on the Cumberland, a distance of two hundred miles; the hardships and perils of which journeys, it is difficult for the modern traveller, in steamboats and stages, to conceive.— Often, with his loaded rifle on his shoulder, his pistols, blanket and provisions strapped to his saddle, the young lawyer might be met on the dangerous route alone. Having to sleep out under the open sky, to ford deep and swollen streams, and not unfrequently to pass whole days without eating, while fat turkeys, and pheasants, and deer were on every side, which he dared not kill, lest the report of his rifle might alarm the lurking savage. Many anecdotes and incidents occurring to our hero at this time, are strongly illustrative of the life of these early Western pioneers.

On one occasion, with three companions, he was on his way from Jonesborough to the settlements on the Cumberland. When arriving, just before dark, on the east side of the Emory, where it issues from the mountains, they saw the fires of a large party of hostile Indians on the opposite bank. The party, by that instinct which discovers who among them is the master mind, immediately put themselves under the guidance of Jackson. He at once led them backwards into the mountains, keep-

ing up the stream, for the purpose of fording it at
some distance above, taking care, however, to leave
no traces by which the Indians might follow them.
They kept up the stream during the whole night,
guided by the noise of its current, and in the morning attempted to ford it, but found that it was too
much swollen to be waded, and too rapid to be
swum. Still fearing pursuit, they kept on until two
o'clock, when they came to a place where the stream
presented a smooth surface, with a cataract below,
and another fall above. Still anxious to get the
river between them and their late trail, they set
about forming a raft. This being constructed from
rude logs, bound together by hickory withes, and
having made two oars, as well as a rudder, they
commenced the passage across. It was cold March
weather, and therefore of the utmost importance to
keep their blankets and saddles, as well as their
rifles and powder, from getting wet. It was concluded, therefore, that Jackson, with one other of
the party, should first carry over all the moveables,
and, returning, they could swim the horses after the
raft. As soon as the raft had been pushed out from
the shore, a strong under-current commenced forc-
ing it toward the falls below. Jackson, regardless
of the admonitions of his companions on the shore,

continued for some time to struggle with his oars against the current, but perceiving that his exertions would be in vain, he at last endeavoured to bring the raft back to the bank from which he had started.

With all his strength he was unable to bring it to land—the suck of the cataract had already seized it. A moment more, and the raft, with its passengers, would have been dashed to pieces,—when Jackson, wrenching one of his oars from its fastenings, sprung to the stern, and bracing himself there, held it out to his companions on the shore, who, fortunately being within reach, seized hold of it and brought the raft to land. Reproached by his companions for not heeding them when they had first warned him, Jackson coolly replied, "a miss is as good as a mile—ye see how I can graze danger—come on, and I will save you yet." Re-equipping themselves, the party resumed their march up the stream; and having spent another night in the woods, supperless, they found a ford next morning —and next day reached a log cabin on their road, about forty miles from the Indian encampment.

On another occasion, he reached the rendezvous of a party at Bean's Station, with which he was to cross the wilderness, the evening after they had left. With the intention of overtaking them, he took a

guide with him, who was well acquainted with Indian traces, and travelled all night. Just before day
he came to the place where his friends had encamped the night previous, and from the traces the
guide discovered that a party of Indians had gone
in pursuit of them. Following on, they came so
near the Indians that the guide refused to go any
further. Jackson was determined to save his
friends or perish; and dividing his provisions with
the guide, he suffered him to return, while he kept
on after the Indians. At length the traces of the
Indians turned to the right from the route which
the travellers had taken. Jackson, rightly conclud-
ing that they had made a circuit, to head the party
and attack them in the night, hastened his speed,
and overtook his friends just before dark. Having
just forded a deep and frozen stream, they were
drying their clothes and warming themselves by the
fires which they had kindled. Taking advice from
Jackson, they resumed their journey, and continued
it during the whole night and the next day. It had
now commenced to snow, and the sky portended a
severe storm. Arriving at the log cabins of some
hunters, they requested shelter and protection during the night. They were, contrary to their expectations, rudely refused. Jackson, wearied with

the journey, and having been two nights without
sleep, wrapped himself in his blanket, and lay down
by the trunk of a large tree, where he slept sound-
ly; and when awaking in the morning, he found
himself covered with six inches of snow. The
party resumed their march, and reached their destination in safety; but they afterwards learned that
the hunters, who had refused them shelter, had been
every one butchered by the Indians who had pursued them.

CHAPTER V.

JACKSON LOCATES HIMSELF PERMANENTLY AT NASHVILLE.—
HIS MARRIAGE.

FTER making several professional visits, back and forth, from Jonesborough to the settlement on the Cumberland, Jackson, wisely judging that Nashville offered tempting inducements to a young lawyer, concluded to make a permanent location in that place.

It had not been Jackson's intention certainly to make Tennessee the place of his future residence; his visit was merely experimental, and his stay remained to be determined by the advantages that might be disclosed: but finding, soon after his arrival, that a considerable opening was offered for the success of a young attorney, he determined to remain. To one of refined feelings, the prospect before him was certainly not of an encouraging cast. As in all newly-settled countries must be the case, society was loosely formed, and united by but few of those ties which have a tendency to enforce the performance of moral duty, and the right execution of justice. The young men of the place, adventurers from different sections of the country, had become indebted to the merchants; there was but one lawyer in the country, and they had so contrived as to retain him in their business; the consequence was, that the merchants were entirely deprived of the means of enforcing against the delinquents the execution of their contracts. In this state of things, Jackson made his appearance at Nashville, and, while the creditor class looked to it with great satisfaction, the debtors were sorely displeased. Applications were immediately made to him for his professional services, and on the morning after his arrival he issued seventy writs. To those prodigal gentlemen it was an alarming circumstance; their former security was impaired; but that it might not wholly depart, they determined to force him, in some way or other, to leave the country; and to effect this, broils and quarrels with him were to be resorted to. This, however, was soon abandoned; satisfied, by the first controversy in which they had involved him, that his decision and firmness were such as to

THE ESCAPE.

leave no hope of effecting anything through this channel.

Frequent expeditions were undertaken from Nashville about this time, against the Indians, in most of which Jackson took part. These continued until 1794, when a large party, among whom was our hero, attacked and destroyed the Indian town of Nickajack, near the Tennessee river.

In these affairs, General Jackson, by his courage and gallantry, had so distinguished himself, as to have obtained the sobriquet of "Sharp Knife" from his tawny foemen. He had also gained the confidence of the hardy hunters whom he accompanied.

When Jackson first located himself in the town of Nashville, hotels and boarding-houses were totally unknown; the stranger or traveller finding himself welcome at the firesides of the hospitable settlers, who, in their turn, were glad of the additional protection thus afforded them from the attacks of the savage Indian.

Jackson and his friend, the late Judge Overton, became boarders in the family of Mrs. Donelson, a widow lady, who had emigrated from Virginia, first to Kentucky, afterwards to Nashville. Mrs. Robards, her daughter, who afterwards became the wife of General Jackson, was then living in the famiiy with her mother. On account of some ιl. treatment which she had received at the hands of her husband, Mrs. Robards had followed her mother to Tennessee. A reconciliation had taken place between Robards and his wife, but had been shortly after followed by a fresh outbreak; and hearing that Robards threatened to carry her back to Kentucky, Mrs. Robards, with the advice of her friends, determined to decend the river as far as Natchez, in company with Colonel Stark, who was then preparing for the voyage. Stark being an elderly man, and apprehensive of danger, invited Jackson to accompany him. Jackson accepted the invitation and after seeing the little party safely to their journey's end, returned to Nashville.

In the meantime, Robards applied for and obtained a divorce; upon hearing which, Jackson returned to Natchez, and having paid his addresses to the lady in question, was accepted. In the fall of 1791 they were married, and returned to Nashville, amid the joyous congratulations of her relatives, and a large circle of mutual friends.

CHAPTER VI.

JACKSON BECOMES A SENATOR IN THE U. S. CONGRESS.—RE
SIGNS.—IS APPOINTED JUDGE OF THE SUPREME COURT

AFTER his marriage, Jackson applied himself assiduously to his profession. But the war which he had waged against the debtors, on his first settling in Nashville, had created many and bitter enemies, who now sought every means to disgrace and annoy him. Personal quarrels were sought with him, and " bullies," a species of characters who were at this time found in great numbers in the Western settlements, were employed to attack him.

While he was attending a court in Sumner County, one of these, instigated no doubt by some enemy of Jackson, approached him in the street, and rudely assaulted him. Jackson pushed the man off to a distance, and laying hold of a slab, thrust him in the breast so forcibly that the bully was brought to the

ground. Recovering, however, he again prepared
for fight. The crowd here interfered to prevent
further conflict, but at the entreaty of Jackson again
stood aside. Poising his slab, with a firm step and
a steady eye, Jackson advanced upon his anta-
gonist, who, at his approach, dropped his weapon,
jumped the fence and took to the woods. The result of a few encounters such as this, freed him ever
after from all such annoyances.

In 1795, the people of Tennessee took measures
for forming a state government, with a view to ad-
mission into the Union. Jackson, without offering
himself as a candidate, was elected as one of the
members of the Convention.

In June, 1796, Tennessee became by an act of
Congress, one of the United States, and on the same
footing with the others. It was only entitled to one
representative in Congress, and General Jackson
was elected as that representative without having
been a candidate. He took his seat in the House
of Representatives on the 5th day of December,
1796. Having served one session as a representative, he was elected to the Senate of the United
States, and took his seat in November, 1797. Unambitious, however, of political distinction, he resigned in one year after his election, and returned
to his home at Nashville.

Soon after, the Legislature of Tennessee conferred upon him the appointment of Judge of the Supreme Court. His first court was held at Jonesborough. An incident occurred during the sitting of this court, which is illustrative, both of the rudeness of the times, and of the firmness of Jackson.

A man named Russel Bean had been indicted for cutting off the ears of his infant child in a drunken frolic. Bean was in the court yard; but, from his well-known ferocity of character, and from his threats to shoot any one who would dare to take him, the sheriff had made the return to the court, that "Russel Bean will not be taken." "He must be taken," said the judge, "and if necessary you can summon the *posse comitatus.*" The mortified sheriff retired, and waiting till the court adjourned for dinner, summoned the judges themselves as part of the *posse.* Conceiving that this was a ruse on the part of the sheriff to avoid a dangerous piece of service, Judge Jackson replied, "Yes sir, I will attend you, and see that you do your duty."— Learning that Bean was armed, Jackson requested a loaded pistol, which was instantly put into his hand. He then said to the sheriff, "Advance, and arrest him—I will protect you from harm!" Bean, armed with a dirk and a brace of pistols, assumed an attitude of defiance; but when the judge drew

near he began to retreat. "Stop, and submit to the
law!" cried the judge. The culprit stopped, threw
down his pistols, and replied, "I will surrender to
you, sir, but to no one else;" and so saying he quietly
permitted himself to be taken prisoner. This conduct of Judge Jackson had a wholesome effect on
the turbulent spirits of the country.

In 1804, Judge Jackson sent in his resignation
to the Legislature, which was accepted by that
body, in July, about six years after his appointment.
Unambitious of those distinctions and honours,
which young men are usually proud to possess, and
finding too that his circumstances and condition in
life were not such as to permit his time and attention to be devoted to public matters, he determined
to yield them into other hands, and to devote himself to agricultural pursuits; and accordingly settled
himself on an excellent farm, ten miles from Nashville, on the Cumberland river; where, for several
years, he enjoyed all the comforts of domestic and
social intercourse. Abstracted from the busy scenes
of public life, pleased with retirement, surrounded
by friends whom he loved, and who entertained for
him the highest veneration and respect, and blessed
with an amiable and affectionate wife, nothing seemed
wanting to the completion of that happiness which
he so anxiously desired while in office

JACKSON AS JUDGE.

CHAPTER VII

FROM HIS RESIGNATION AS JUDGE TILL 1812.

REVIOUS to the resignation of Jackson as Judge, he had been elected Major-General of the Tennessee militia; which office, as it did not much interfere with his domestic pursuits, he still continued to hold.

During his residence upon his farm, one of his favourite employments was in the raising of fine cattle; and though not an enthusiastic sportsman, he brought out his favourite horses upon the race-courses of the day.

An unfortunate quarrel, about a bet upon one of these match-races, occurred between him and a Mr. Charles Dickinson, which resulted in a duel. In the duel Dickinson, who had borne the character of a crack-shot and duellist, was killed. There are few, however, except the immediate friends of Dickinson, who attach any blame to Jackson,—as, under the

provocation which he had received from the former
and considering the state of society as it existed in
Tennessee at this time, it would have been impossible for him to avoid the encounter. It is
said that Dickinson, previous to the duel, had been
making bets that he would. kill him, and boasting
how often he had hit the general chalked out upon
a tree. He did in fact hit General Jackson in the
duel, but fortunately the ball, lodging in his breast,
did not penetrate. Two of his ribs were shattered
near the breast-bone. Jackson had gone upon the
ground with the full conviction that his life was
eagerly sought, and with the expectation of losing
it; but his was a bosom that never knew fear.

Shortly after this, General Jackson entered into
partnership with a merchant in Nashville—though
he took no active part in the business himself. After
a time, however, he began to suspect that the business was not going on right, and upon demanding a
full investigation, he found that his partner, in
whom he had placed the utmost confidence, had
already involved him for many thousand dollars of
debts. He closed the business, sold the fine plantation upon which he lived, and paying off his debts
with the proceeds of the sale, he retired into a log
cabin, to begin the world anew. From the humble

dwelling, into which he had moved, he could see the fine house and plantation so lately his own—admonishing him of the danger of connection with others in business, and of the contracting of debts.

It was not long, however, before he became **comfortable in the world.***

CHAPTER VIII.

ADVENTURE WITH THE INDIAN AGENT.

N the year 1811, Jackson had occasion to travel to Natchez on business. The road from Nashville to the former place passed through the Choctaw and Chickasaw nations, and there was an Indian agent for the Choctaws stationed upon it. On arriving at this station, General Jackson found some seven or eight families detained here, as well as two members of the Mississippi Legislative Council, by the agent, upon the plea that they had no passports. They were remaining there until their passports could reach them, one of their number having gone back for the purpose of procuring them. Some of the persons thus prevented from executing their journey, were purchasing corn from the agent to feed their cattle, at a very high price, and had been employed by him to split rails at a very low price.

When Jackson understood these things, he became very angry, and reproached the two members
for submitting to such treatment at the hands of the
mercenary agent. The agent hearing this, inquired
in an impertinent manner if he had a pass. "Yes,
sir," said Jackson; "I always carry my passport
with me when I travel: I am a free American citizen,
and that is a passport all over the world." "We
shall see," said the agent. "Very well, we *shall*
see," was the reply of Jackson; and calling upon
the wagoners to gear up their wagons, and shoot
any one down who should attempt to obstruct them,
he led the whole party away.

On his return, however, he understood that the
agent had collected about one hundred and fifty
men, white and Indian, to stop him, unless he procured a passport. He would not, though advised
by his friends, procure one, believing as he said, that
no American citizen should submit to the insult of
carrying a pass to enable him to travel through his
own country. He double armed himself, however,
prepared for any emergency; and, on nearing the
station of the agent, he put axes and other arms
into the hands of a number of blacks, whom he was
carrying from Natchez to the upper country, telling
them how and when to use them. As had been re-

ported, the agent had collected a goodly number of men to stop him. Jackson approached, and upon the agent's asking him whether he meant to stop and show his passport, Jackson replied, "That depends on circumstances; I am told that you mean to stop me by force; whoever attempts such a thing will not have long to live!" His determined manner had such an effect, that the agent was glad to let him pass on quietly. The Indians, whose chiefs were acquainted with Jackson, "Sharp Knife," now approached and shook hands with him; and those bold sons of the forest were so much struck with his courage, that if he had only commanded it, they would have turned round and scalped the agent in his stead. He afterwards reported the conduct of the agent to government, and he was dismissed from nis agency.

CHAPTER IX

WAR OF 1812.—EXPEDITION TO NATCHEZ.

E now come to that period in the life of General Jackson, when his great military talents, that had hitherto remained unemployed, and in fact unknown, were to be called into action.

The government of the United States, after patiently submitting to many insults and injuries from Great Britain, declared war against that country in the month of June, 1812.

Jackson at this time, happy on his farm, and retired, as he apparently thought, for ever, from all public affairs—though only forty-five years of age —was again roused by the insults offered to his country, by the wrongs inflicted upon her citizens, and by the recollection, no doubt, of the death of his mother, of the death of his brother Robert, of the cause of those deaths; and, if he could have forgotten the horrid account of the injuries inflicted upon the country of his father and his mother, there was that scar on his hand, inflicted by a British officer, who had aimed a blow at his life because he had refused to clean the dirt off his boots; there was that scar to keep his virtuous resentment alive, even if he could have forgotten the wrongs of Ireland, and the ruin or extermination of every relation in the world.

In answer to a spirited address from him, 2500 volunteers flocked to his standard—prepared to follow wheresoever he might see fit to lead them. He received orders to place himself at their head, and to descend the Mississippi, for the defence of the lower country, which was then supposed to be in danger. Accordingly, on the 10th of December, 1812, those troops rendezvoused at Nashville, prepared to advance to the place of their destination; and although the weather was then excessively severe, and the ground covered with snow, no troops could have displayed greater firmness.

Having procured supplies, and made the necessary arrangements for an active campaign, they proceeded, the 7th of January, 1813, on their journey; and descending the Ohio and Mississippi

through cold and ice, arrived and halted at
Natchez. Here Jackson had been instructed to
remain until he should receive further orders. Having chosen a healthful site for the encampment of his
troops, he devoted his time, with the utmost industry, to training and preparing them for active service. The clouds of war, however, in that quarter,
having blown over, an order was received from the
secretary of war, dated 5th of January, 1813, di-
recting him, on the receipt thereof, to dismiss those
under his command from service, and to take measures for delivering over every article of public property in his possession to Brigadier-general Wilkinson. When this order reached his camp, there
were one hundred and fifty on the sick report, fifty-
six of whom were unable to raise their heads, and
almost the whole of them destitute of the means of
defraying the expenses of their return. The consequence of a strict compliance with the secretary's
order inevitably would have been, that many of the
sick must have perished; while most of the others,
from their destitute condition, would, of necessity,
have been compelled to enlist in the regular army,
under General Wilkinson.

Jackson was, as a matter of course, very much
astonished at the reception of such an order, the

consequence of obeying which, he clearly saw, would be the death of many of the brave young men whom he had brought with him from Tennessee, and to whom he had given his promise, before they had left their homes, that he would be to them as a father and the guardian of their welfare.

He saw, moreover, that the design of the order had been a concerted thing, between the secretary of war, Armstrong, and General Wilkinson, commandant of the United States regular army in the south-western department—who by this means expected to recruit largely from among these young men, who, now, unable to return home, would be obliged to enter the ranks of the regular army. Moreover, General Wilkinson was jealous of Jackson, whose authority as major-general was equal to his own, if not greater, and their commands were likely to interfere with each other. Under these circumstances, Jackson determined to disobey the orders of the secretary.

Having made known his resolution to the field-officers of his division, it met, apparently, their approbation; but, after retiring from his presence, they assembled late at night, in secret caucus, and proceeded to recommend to him an abandonmen* of his purpose, and an immediate discharge of his troops. Great as was the astonishment which this measure excited in the General, it produced a still higher sentiment of indignation. In reply, he urged the duplicity of their conduct, and reminded them, that although to those who possessed funds and health such a course could produce no inconvenience, yet to the unfortunate soldier, who was alike destitute of both, no measure could be more calamitous. He concluded by telling them that his resolution, not having been hastily concluded on, nor founded on light considerations, was unalterably fixed; and that immediate preparations must be made for carrying into execution the determination he had formed.

During these negotiations, the officers of General Wilkinson had arrived in the camp, with the intention of recruiting from the volunteer army. As soon as Jackson became apprised of this, he gave orders, that any officer found recruiting from among his troops, that were already in the service of the United States, should be arrested and confined. The quarter-master had been ordered to provide the means for transporting the sick and baggage, and pretended to be making these necessary arrangements. To keep up the appearance of doing so, and the better to deceive, he had ordered a number

of wagons into the camp. The next morning, how
ever, when everything was about to be packed up,
acting doubtless by orders from Wilkinson, and intending to produce embarrassment, the quarter-
master entered the encampment, and discharged the
whole. He was grossly mistaken in the man he
had to deal with, and had now played his tricks too
far to be able to accomplish the object which he had,
no doubt, been instructed to effect. Disregarding
their dismissal, so evidently designed to prevent his
marching back his men, General Jackson seized
upon these wagons, yet within his lines, and compelled them to proceed to the transportation of his
sick. It deserves to be recollected that this quarter
master, so soon as he received directions for fur-
nishing transportation, had despatched an express
to General Wilkinson; and there can be but little
doubt, that the course of duplicity he afterwards
pursued was a concerted plan, between him and that
general, to defeat the design of Jackson, compel him
to abandon the course he had adopted, and in this
way draw to the regular army many of the soldiers,
who, from necessity, would be driven to enlist. In
this attempt they were fortunately disappointed.
Adhering to his original purpose, he successfully
resisted every stratagem of Wilkinson and marched

the whole of his division to the section of country whence they had been drawn, and dismissed them from service, as he had been instructed.

The conduct of General Jackson in this affair, wrong as it at first appeared, was in the end approved by the government. Every man, whose heart is the seat of justice, will applaud him for stubbornly resisting these crafty suggestions of envy; and it should be told here, that Armstrong, who gave the order for this act of oppression, was disgraced and degraded, not many months afterward, for his scandalous neglect to prepare for the defence of the city of Washington, where he was residing; and that Wilkinson, who was appointed to put the order into execution, and to supplant Jackson, was sufficiently disgraced, in less than two years from that day, on the confines of Canada.

CHAPTER X.

THE INDIAN CAMPAIGN.

HE repose of General Jackson and his volunteers, was not of long duration. After his return from Natchez, the Indian nations scattered over the country, now called Alabama and Mississippi, had begun to harass the frontier settlements; and instigated by the celebrated chief, Tecumseh, as well as secretly encouraged by the British government, threatened a general rising and massacre of the whites on their borders. The Creeks, residing in Alabama, near the Coosa and Tallapoosa rivers, were the most hostile of all these tribes.

There was a large number of these Indians, particularly the old men, who advocated peace and alliance with the United States government; but these were, in the end, obliged to give up, many of them losing their lives in a kind of civil war which ensued. Through a system of false prophets whicn Tecumseh had succeeded in establishing, these deluded savages were taught to believe that the time had come when the white race were to be exterminated.

Fort Mimms, situated in the Tensaw settlement n the Mississippi territory, was the first point designed to satiate their cruelty and vengeance. It contained, at that time, about one hundred and fifty men, under the command of Major Beasley, besides a considerable number of women and children, who had betaken themselves to it for security. Having collected a supply of ammunition from the Spaniards at Pensacola, and assembled their warriors to the number of six or seven hundred, the war party, commanded by Weatherford, a distinguished chief of the nation, on the 30th of August, 1813, commenced their assault on the fort; and having succeeded in carrying it, put to death nearly three hundred persons, including women and children, with the most savage barbarity. The slaughter was indiscriminate; mercy was extended to none; and the tomahawk, at the same stroke, often cleft the mother and the child. But seventeen of the whole number in the fort escaped to bring intelligence of the dreadful catastrophe. This monstrous and un provoked outrage no sooner reached Tennessee than the whole state was thrown into a ferment, and nothing was thought or spoken of but retaliatory vengeance.

It is unnecessary to detail the proceedings of General Jackson after the receipt of this disastrous news. By the order of his government, he immediately called out the militia and volunteers to the number of 2500, and on the 10th of October reached Huntsville, on his line of march towards the Creek country. At the same time, an equal force under General Cocke had been ordered from East Tennessee; while another was despatched from Georgia under Major Floyd, to enter the Indian country on the east; and a regiment of United States' soldiers, with the volunteers of Mississippi under General Claiborne, were to attack the hostile nations on the west.

In consequence of the failure of army contractors to supply provisions, without which it was utterly impossible to proceed, General Jackson was detained for nearly a month in the neighbourhood of the Tennessee river, without being able to penetrate the hostile territory, and strike a decisive blow. General Cocke, who was under a promise to furnish provisions, as well as under orders to unite with

Jackson, kept aloof from motives of jealousy
Jackson had established his head quarters on the
Coosa, at a place called "Ten Islands," where he
erected a fort and depôt, to be called "Fort Strother."

Learning now that a considerable body of the
enemy had posted themselves at Tallushatchee, on
the south side of the Coosa, about thirteen miles
distant, General Coffee was detached with nine
hundred men (the mounted troops having been previously organized into a brigade, and placed under
his command) to attack and disperse them. With
this force he was enabled, through the direction of
an Indian pilot, to ford the Coosa at the Fish-dams,
about four miles above the islands; and having encamped beyond it, very early the next morning proceeded to the execution of his order. Having arrived within a mile and a half, he formed his detachment into two divisions, and directed them to march
so as to encircle the town, by uniting their fronts
beyond it. The enemy, hearing of his approach,
began to prepare for action, which was announced
by the beating of drums, mingled with their savage
yells and war-whoops. An hour after sunrise, the
action was commenced by Captain Hammond's and
Lieutenant Patterson's companies of spies, who had
gone within the circle of alignement for the purpose

of drawing the Indians from their buildings. No sooner had these companies exhibited their front in view of the town, and given a few scattering shot, than the enemy formed, and made a violent charge. Being compelled to give way, the advance-guard were pursued until they reached the main body of the army, which immediately opened a general fire, and charged in their turn. The Indians retreated, firing, until they got around and in their buildings, where an obstinate conflict ensued, and where those who maintained their ground, persisted in fighting as long as they could stand or sit, without manifesting fear or soliciting quarter. Their loss was a hundred and eighty-six killed; among whom were, unfortunately, and through accident, a few women and children. Eighty-four women and children were taken prisoners, towards whom the utmost humanity was shown. Of the Americans, five were killed, and forty-one wounded. Two were killed with arrows, which on this occasion formed a principal part of the arms of the Indians; each one having a bow and quiver, which he used after the first fire of his gun, until an opportunity occurred for reloading.

Having buried his dead, and provided for his wounded, General Coffee, late in the evening of the

same day united with the main army, bringing with
him about forty prisoners; of the residue, a part
were too badly wounded to be removed, and were,
therefore, left with a sufficient number to take care
of them. Those whom he brought in, received
every comfort and assistance their situation demanded, and for safety were immediately sent into
the settlements.

From the manner in which the enemy fought, the
killing and wounding others than their warriors
could not be avoided. On their retreat to their
village, after the commencement of the battle, they
resorted to their block-houses and strong log dwell-
ings, whence they kept up resistance, and for a long
time protracted the fight. Thus mingled with their
women and children it was impossible to prevent
numbers of the latter from falling a sacrifice, and
many were injured, though every precaution was
taken to prevent it. In fact, many of the women
united with their warriors, and contended in the
battle with a fearless and heroic bravery worthy of
the Helvetian matrons.

A pleasing incident in the life of General Jackson,
is recorded in connection with the destruction of
Tallushatchee. Among the slain was found an
Indian woman with an infant, a boy, unhurt, sucking

her lifeless breast. The little orphan was carried to
camp along with other prisoners, and General Jackson tried to hire some of the captive Indian women
to take care of him. They obstinately refused, saying: "All his people dead—kill him too." There
was a little sugar still left in the camp, and with this
the babe was nourished, until he could be sent to a
nurse at Huntsville, which was afterwards done.
Upon General Jackson's return home, he took the
babe with him, and with the cordial aid of Mrs.
Jackson, raised him as tenderly as if he had been
his own son. He named the boy Lincoyer, and
gave him an education equal to that of the white
boys of the most respectable families. Lincoyer
grew up a strong and handsome young man, yet his
tastes were always Indian. He delighted in rambling
away, into the forest, and ornamenting himself with
gay and brilliant feathers, and when the chiefs of
the Creek nation would visit the Hermitage, (the
residence of General Jackson,) which they often did
after the war, he never saw them depart without
sighing to return to the wild forest land of his
nativity.

At length General Jackson carried him to Nashville and desired him to select a trade. He was
best pleased with the saddlers' business, to which he

was bound an apprentice. He continued to work for some time at his trade, paying regular visits to the Hermitage on Saturdays, and returning to his duty on Monday morning. His health, however, began to decline, and General Jackson took him home to his own house, where he was most tenderly waited on, both by himself and Mrs. Jackson, but in vain. He sank rapidly into a consumption, which ended his short career ere he had reached the age of manhood. He was mourned by the General and Mrs. Jackson as though they had lost a favourite son, and was ever after spoken of by them with parental affection.

CHAPTER XI.

BATTLE OF TALLADEGA.

S yet no certain intelligence was received of any collection of the enemy. The army was busily engaged in fortifying and strengthening the site fixed on for a depot, to which the name of Fort Strother had been given. Late, however, on the evening of the 7th November, a runner arrived from Talladega, a fort of the friendly Indians, distant about thirty miles below, with information that the enemy had that morning encamped before it in great numbers, and would certainly destroy it unless immediate assistance could be afforded. Jackson, confiding in the statement, determined to lose no time in extending the relief which was solicited.

Accordingly he issued marching orders, and crossed the Coosa river, at midnight on the 7th of November, with his whole disposable force, con-

sisting of 1200 infantry and 800 cavalry. Next
evening his army lay within six miles of Talladega.
Next morning he marched against the enemy, who
were encamped at the distance of a quarter of a
mile from the fort which they were besieging.
About eight o'clock, A. M., the advance having
arrived within eighty yards of the enemy, who were
concealed in a thick shrubbery that covered the
margin of a small rivulet, received a heavy fire,
which they instantly returned with much spirit.
Falling in with the enemy, agreeably to their in-
structions, they retired towards the centre, but not
before they had dislodged them from their position.
The Indians, now screaming and yelling hideously,
rushed forward in the direction of General Roberts
brigade, a few companies of which, alarmed by their
numbers and yells, gave way at the first fire. Jackson, to fill the chasm which was thus created, directed the regiment commanded by Colonel Bradley
to be moved up, which, from some unaccountable
cause, had failed to advance in a line with the
others, and now occupied a position in rear of the
centre: Bradley, however, to whom this order was
given by one of the staff, omitted to execute it in
time, alleging he was determined to remain on the
eminence which he then possessed until he should

be approached and attacked by the enemy. Owing to this failure in the volunteer regiment, it became necessary to dismount the reserve, which, with great firmness, met the approach of the enemy, who were rapidly moving in this direction. The retreating militia, somewhat mortified at seeing their places so promptly supplied, rallied, and, recovering their former position in the line, aided in checking the advance of the savages. The action now became general along the line, and in fifteen minutes the Indians were seen flying in every direction. On the left they were met and repulsed by the mounted riflemen; but on the right, owing to the halt of Bradley's regiment, which was intended to occupy the extreme right, and to the circumstance of Colonel Allcorn, who commanded one of the wings of the cavalry, having taken too large a circuit, a considerable space was left between the infantry and the cavalry, through which numbers escaped. The fight was maintained with great spirit and effect on both sides, as well before as after the retreat commenced; nor did the pursuit and slaughter terminate until the mountains were reached, at the distance of three miles.

In this battle, the force of the enemy was one thousand and eighty, of whom two hundred and ninety-nine were left dead on the ground; and it is believed that many were killed in the flight, who were not found when the estimate was made. Probably few escaped unhurt. Their loss on this occasion, as stated since by themselves, was not less than six hundred: that of the Americans was fifteen killed and eighty wounded, several of whom afterward died. Jackson, after collecting his dead and wounded, advanced his army beyond the fort, and encamped for the night. The Indians who had been for several days shut up by the besiegers, thus fortunately liberated from the most dreadful apprehensions and severest privations, having for some time been entirely without water, received the army with all the demonstrations of gratitude that savages could give. Their manifestations of joy for their deliverance presented an interesting and affecting spectacle. Their fears had been already greatly excited, for it was the very day when they were to have been assaulted, and when every soul within the **fort must have perished.**

CHAPTER XII.

N account of the want of provisions, Jackson was unable to follow up the successful blow struck at Talladega, and was compelled to retreat to Fort Strother. But on his arrival here, he found that through the stupid mismanagement, and perhaps jealousy of General Cocke, no supplies had arrived even here, and the soldiers now began to show signs of discontent.

A few dozen biscuits, which remained on his return, were given to hungry applicants, without being tasted by himself or family, who were probably not less hungry than those who were thus relieved. A scanty supply of indifferent beef, taken from the enemy or purchased of the Cherokees, was now the only support afforded. Thus left destitute, Jackson, with the u most cheerfulness of temper, repaired to

JACKSON AND THE ACORNS.

the bullock-pen, and of the offal there thrown away, provided for himself and staff what he was pleased to call, and seemed really to think, a very comfortable repast. Tripes, however, hastily provided in a camp, without bread or seasoning, can only be palatable to an appetite very highly whetted; yet this constituted for several days the only diet at head-quarters, during which time the General seemed entirely satisfied with his fare. Neither this nor the liberal donations by which he disfurnished himself to relieve the suffering soldier, deserves to be ascribed to osten tation or design: the one flowed from benevolence, the other from necessity, and a desire to place before his men an example of patience and suffering which he felt might be necessary, and hoped might be serviceable. Of these two imputations no human being, invested with rank and power, was ever more deservedly free. Charity in him was a warm and active propensity of the heart, urging him, by an instantaneous impulse, to relieve the wants of the distressed, without regarding, or even thinking of, the consequences. Many of those to whom it was extended had no conception of the source that supplied them, and believed the comforts they received were, indeed, drawn from stores provided for the nospital department.

E

On this campaign, a soldier one morning, with a wo-begone countenance, approached the General, stating that he was nearly starved, that he had nothing to eat, and could not imagine what he should do. He was the more encouraged to complain, from perceiving that the General, who had seated himself at the root of a tree, waiting the coming up of the rear of the army, was busily engaged in eating something. The poor fellow was impressed with the belief, from what he saw, that want only attached to the soldiers; and that the officers, particularly the General, were liberally and well supplied. He accordingly approached him with great confidence of being relieved; Jackson told him that it had always been a rule with him never to turn away a hungry man when it was in his power to relieve him. "I will most cheerfully," said he, "divide with you what I have;" and putting his hand to his pocket, drew forth a few acorns, from which he had been feasting, adding, it was the best and only fare he had. The soldier seemed much surprised, and forthwith circulated among his com rades that their General was actually subsisting upon acorns, and that they ought hence no more to complain. From this circumstance was derived the story heretofore published to the world, that Jackson, about the period of his greatest suffering, and with a view to inspirit them, had invited his officers to dine with him, and presented for their repast water and a tray of acorns.

Notwithstanding the firmness and patriotism of their general, the army, consisting entirely of volun‑teers and militia, now unable for want of provisions to penetrate the hostile territory, became anxious to return to their homes, and from a misunderstanding with regard to the term of service for which they had been enlisted, they believed that the time had expired. This was not so; and Jackson, deeply anxious to finish successfully the campaign, resolved to prevent such a disgraceful abandonment. Several times did the troops mutiny, and as often were they brought back to their duty by the talents and bravery of their general. One of these scenes may be presented as a specimen of the iron firmness of our hero.

He had promised his army that unless supplies arrived on a certain day, he would grant their re‑quest to return. The supplies did not arrive until they had commenced their march homeward, when they were met by one hundred and fifty beeves. This, of course, relieved Jackson from his promise, but so great was the aversion of his men to return 'to the camp, that they preferred breaking their word of honour. One company was already moving off in a direction towards home. They had proceeded some distance before information of their departure was had by Jackson. Irritated at their conduct, in attempting to violate the promise they had given, and knowing that the success of future operations depended on the result, the General pursued, until he came near a part of his staff and a few soldiers, who, with General Coffee, had halted about a quarter of a mile ahead. He ordered them to form immediately across the road, and to fire on the mutineers if they attempted to proceed. Snatching up their arms, these faithful adherents presented a front which threw the deserters into affright, and caused them to retreat precipitately to the main body. Here it was hoped the matter would end, and that no further opposition would be made to returning. This expectation was not realized; a mutinous temper began presently to display itself throughout the whole brigade. Jackson, having left his aid-de-camp, Major Reid, engaged in making up some despatches, had gone out alone among his troops, who were at some distance; on his arrival he found a much more extensive mutiny than that which had just been quelled. Almost the whole brigade had put itself into an attitude for moving forcibly off. A crisis had arrived; and, feeling its importance, he determined to take no middle ground. but to triumph or perish. He was still without the use of his left arm, but, seizing a musket, and resting it on the neck of his horse, he threw himself in front of the column, and threatened to shoot the first man who should attempt to advance. In this situation he was found by Major Reid and General Coffee; who, fearing, from the length of his absence, that some disturbance had arisen, hastened where he was, and placing themselves by his side, awaited the result in anxious expectation. For many minutes the column preserved a sullen, yet hesitating attitude, fearing to proceed in their purpose, and disliking to abandon it. In the mean time, those who remained faithful to their duty, amounting to about two companies, were collected and formed at a short distance in advance of the troops and in rear of the General, with positive directions to imitate his example in firing if they attempted to proceed. At length, finding n > one bold enough to advance, and overtaken by those fears which in the hour of peril always beset persons engaged in what they know to be a bad cause, they abandoned their purpose, and turning quietly round, agreed to return to their posts.

Notwithstanding these efforts on the part of the General to detain them, the mutiny was not quelled, and they all looked forward to the 10th of December as the day on which they would be discharged. It will be recollected, that upon this day, twelve months ago, they had been enlisted to proceed to New Orleans, and as they had entered for a service of twelve months, they expected to be discharged at the end of that time, although they had not actually seen twelve months' service, having been discharged after their return from New Orleans. The volunteers, through several of their officers, were pressing on the consideration of the General the expiration of their service, and claiming to be discharged on the 10th of the month. From the colonel who commanded the second regiment he received a letter, dated the 4th of December, 1813, in which was attempted to be detailed their whole ground of complaint. He began by stating, that painful as it was he nevertheless felt himself bound to disclose an important and unpleasant truth: that, on the 10th, the service would be deprived of the regiment he commanded. He seemed to deplore, with great sensibility, the scene that would be exhibited on that day, should opposition be made to their departure; and still more sensibly, the consequences that would

result from a disorderly abandonment of the camp
He stated they had all considered themselves finally
discharged on the 20th of April, 1813, and never
knew to the contrary until they saw his order of the
24th of September, 1813, requiring them to rendezvous at Fayetteville on the 4th of October, 1813;
for the first time, they then learned that they owed
further services, their discharge to the contrary
notwithstanding. "Thus situated, there was considerable opposition to the order; on which the
officers generally, as I am advised, and I know
myself in particular, gave it as an unequivocal
opinion that their term of service would terminate
on the 10th of December, 1813.

"They therefore look to their general, who has
their confidence, for an honourable discharge on
that day; and that, in every respect, he will see that
justice be done them. They regret that their particular situations and circumstances require them to
leave their general at a time when their services are
important to the common cause. It would be de-
sirable," he continued, "that those men who have
served with honour should be honourably discharged,
and that they should return to their families and
friends without even the semblance of disgrace,
with their general they leave it to place them in that

situation. They have received him as an affectionate father, while they have honoured, revered, and obeyed him; but, having devoted a considerable portion of their time to the service of their country, by which their domestic concerns are greatly de ranged, they wish to return, and attend to their own affairs."

To this letter General Jackson returned a reply, which for firmness of resolution, and patriotic devotion to the cause of his country, and to the cause of right, never was surpassed by the address of a great commander to a blind and mutinous army. He declared his determination to prevent their return at the hazard of his own life, and called upon God to witness that the scenes of blood which might be exhibited upon that day should not be laid to his charge. His address concludes with the following remarkable words:

"I cannot, must not, believe that the 'Volunteers of Tennessee,' a name ever dear to fame, will disgrace themselves, and a country which they have honoured, by abandoning her standard, as mutineers and deserters; but should I be disappointed and compelled to resign this pleasing hope, one thing I will not resign—*my duty.* Mutiny and sedition, as long as I possess the power of quelling them, shall

be put down; and even when left destitute of this, I
will still be found, in the last extremity, endeavouring
to discharge the duty which I owe to my country
and myself."

To the platoon officers, who addressed him on
the same subject, he replied with nearly the same
spirited feeling; but discontent was too deeply
fastened, and by designing men had been too artfully
fomented, to be removed by anything like argument
or entreaty. At length, on the evening of the 9th
of December, 1813, General Hall hastened to the
tent of Jackson, with information that his whole
brigade was in a state of mutiny, and making preparations to move forcibly off. This was a measure
which every consideration of policy, duty and honour
required Jackson to oppose; and to this purpose he
instantly applied all the means he possessed. He
immediately issued the following general order:—
" The commanding general being informed that an
actual mutiny exists in his camp, all officers and
soldiers are commanded to put it down. The
officers and soldiers of the first brigade will, without
delay, parade on the west side of the fort, and await
further orders." The artillery company, with two
small field-pieces, being posted in the front and
rear, and the militia, under the command of Colonel

Wynne, on the eminences, in advance, were ordered to prevent any forcible departure of the volunteers.

The General rode along the line, which had been previously formed agreeably to his orders, and addressed them, by companies, in a strain of impassioned eloquence. He feelingly expatiated on their former good conduct, and the esteem and applause it had secured them; and pointed to the disgrace which they must heap upon themselves, their families, and country, by persisting, even if they could succeed, in their present mutiny. He told them, however, they should not succeed, but by passing over his body; that even in opposing their mutinous spirit, he should perish honourably—by perishing at his post, and in the discharge of his duty. "Reinforcements," he continued, "are preparing to hasten to my assistance; it cannot be long before they will arrive. I am, too, in daily expectation of receiving information whether you may be discharged or not —until then, you must not and shall not retire. I have done with entreaty,—it has been used long enough. I will attempt it no more. You must now determine whether you will go or peaceably remain; if you still persist in your determination to move forcibly off, the point between us shall soon be decided." At first they hesitated: he demanded an explicit and positive answer. They still hesitated, and he commanded the artillerists to prepare the match; he himself remaining in front of the volunteers, and within the line of fire, which he intended soon to order. Alarmed at his apparent determination, and dreading the consequences involved in such a contest, " Let us return," was presently lisped along the line, and soon after determined upon. The officers now came forward and pledged themselves for their men, who either nodded assent or openly expressed a willingness to retire to their quarters and remain without further tumult, until information were had, or the expected aid should arrive. Thus passed away a moment of the greatest peril, and pregnant with important consequences.

This matchless and ever memorable scene, the reader will observe, took place on the 10th of December, 1813; the volunteers having formed their first rendezvous, as he will recollect, on the 10th of December, 1812. *One year* had certainly expired; but there had not been a year's *service;* for they had not been in service from the 1st of May to the 10th of October, 1813; so that there remained five months of the year's service to come. The General was right in his construction of the bargain; but, besides this, to have forsaken the campaign in such a manner would have been ruinous in the extreme. The savage enemy, not yet subdued, but exasperated to the last degree, would have assailed the frontier settlements and deluged them in blood.

Notwithstanding all General Jackson's firmness, however, the want of supplies and the actual need of his army, compelled him reluctantly to allow them to return home, remaining, himself, with about 100 faithful soldiers, in the garrison of Fort Strother, there to await new reinforcements.

CHAPTER XIII.

BATTLES OF EMUCKFAW AND ENOTOCHOPCO.

ABOUT the middle of January, 800 new recruits reached Jackson's camp at Fort Strother. With these it would have been madness to have penetrated the Creek country, but as Jackson rightly conjectured that Major Floyd (who, it will be recollected, by the plan of the campaign, had entered the Indian country from Georgia,) might be closely pressed by the enemy, now that he had failed to co-operate with the Tennessee army, he determined to make with his 800 men a diversion in his favour.

Hearing, from authentic sources, that a large force of the " red-sticks," or hostile Indians, were collected on the Emuckfaw Creek, in a bend of the Tallapoosa River, he thither directed his march, and on the evening of the 21st of January he encamped within a short distance of the enemy. A friendly Indian spy, who had reconnoitred the enemy's camp, brought in word that the Indians were removing their women and children; a sure sign that they meditated an attack. It fell out as he had anticipated.

Early in the morning of the 22d, before day, a brisk firing was heard upon the right, and immediately the engagement became general. The enemy were repulsed with the loss of many of their best warrriors; but the evident strength which they had exhibited, and the fact that they were still continuing to receive fresh reinforcements, determined General Jackson to march back to Fort Strother. He had now accomplished his object, which was to create a diversion in favour of Floyd and the Georgian army; and, as it became known afterwards, the battle of Emuckfaw was probably the means of saving the Georgia troops, who were hotly engaged on the 27th, and with a little more strength on the part of their enemy would have been destroyed.

Having spent the remainder of the 22d in burying the dead, the army marched on the 23d from the ground of Emuckfaw. During the night of the 23d there came on a hurricane, which is always favourable to the fighting of Indians, and as his

troops were not attacked, either in the night or
during their march on the 23d, General Jackson
rightly guessed that the enemy had made up their
minds to lay in ambush for him at the ford of Enotochopco, about twelve miles from Emuckfaw. Here
the stream runs through a deep and dangerous defile,
the ford is deep, and the banks covered with under-
wood and reeds, affording the best shelter for a
lurking foe. Jackson, who had observed these
things when he crossed before, at once resolved to
lead his army over by a ford six hundred yards
lower down. Expecting that the enemy, as soon as
they discovered that he had chosen another route,
would attack him in the rear, he formed his rear so
as to receive them. It turned out as the General
had anticipated. Part of the army had crossed the
creek, the wounded were over, and the artillery were
just entering, when an alarm gun was heard in the
rear, and the next instant the whooping and yelling
of the savages told that they were coming on in
fearful numbers. The militia upon the right and
the left, with their colonels at their head, being
struck with a sudden panic, instantly retreated
down the bank, leaving the brave General Carrol,
with about twenty-five men, to check the advancing
savages. Colonel Stump came plunging down the

bank, meeting General Jackson, who had been on the water's edge superintending the crossing of the artillery. Jackson made an unsuccessful attempt to draw his sword and cut the retreating coward down. Lieutenant Armstrong ordered his company of artillery to form upon the hill, at the same time, with the assistance of one or two others, dragging up the cannon, a six-pounder, and pointing it towards the advancing savages. The ramrod and picker had been lost, and also two gunners, Perkins and Craven. Jackson supplied the deficiency, using their muskets and ramrods to load it. Twice was the little gun fired, and did fearful execution among the Indians. This succeeded in checking the advancing enemy, and in the meantime Jackson had recalled a number of the panic-struck fugitives, who returned to the fight. The savages, perceiving the balance of the army coming up, precipitately fled, throwing away their packs, and leaving twenty-six of their warriors dead upon the field. But for the bravery of Lieutenant Armstrong and General Carrol, the little army would have fallen a sacrifice to the cowardice of Colonels Stump and Perkins. The former was tried by a court-martial and cashiered.

The army reached Fort Strother on the 27th

when they were honourably dismissed by their General, until further orders from the government. He now waited for a competent force to enter into the heart of the Creek country, and put an end to the war.

CHAPTER XIV.

BATTLE OF TOHOPEKA, OR HORSE-SHOE.

N the month of March, thanks to the exertions of Governor Blount, General Jackson was again at the head of a fine army, and ready to recommence the campaign. This force consisted of 4000 Tennessee militia and volunteers, and a regiment of United States regulars.

In the month of February, he received information that the hostile Indians were fortifying themselves in a bend of the Tallapoosa River, called Tohopeka or Horse-shoe, where they had determined to make a last stand. This was exactly what Jackson desired, knowing that if he could get the enemy into a general engagement, he would soon cause them to sue for peace. The country between the Coosa and Tallapoosa rivers, near their junction, known to the whites as the "Hickory Ground," had always been considered by the Indians

as sacred ground, and they believed, being so taught
by their prophets, that no white man could ever
enter this territory to conquer it. The place where
they were now concentrated was in this Hickory
Ground, about fifty miles from Emuckfaw, and in a
bend of the Tallapoosa River. General Jackson
with his army marched down the Coosa, and establishing a fort at the mouth of Cedar Creek,
crossed over to the Tallapoosa. The way had to
be cut from one river to the other, and the army
was three days in crossing the Hickory Ground.
He arrived near Tohopeka on the morning of the
27th, having with him over 2000 men.

The plan of this battle may be easily understood.
The bend of the river in which the enemy was
fortified, as its name imports, resembles in shape a
horse-shoe. Across the neck of land by which it
was entered from the north, the Indians had thrown
up a rude breastwork of logs, seven or eight feet
high, but so constructed that assailants would be
exposed to a double and cross fire. About a hundred
acres lay in this bend, and at the bottom of it was
an Indian village. All around the village, on the
same side of the river, were Indian canoes in great
numbers, fastened to the bank. About 1000 warriors were here assembled.

After seeing how matters stood, Jackson despatched General Coffee to surround the bend opposite to where the canoes were tied, while he himself advanced to assault the breastwork. As soon as Coffee, by signals, had reported that the bend was completely surrounded by his troops, the two pieces of artillery, a six and three-pounder, began to play upon the breastwork. This continued for about two hours, when some of the Cherokees (friendly Indians,) who lay with Coffee on the river edge, round the bend, observing that none of the warriors had been left to guard the canoes, swam across the river and brought them over. In these a number of those under Coffee's command crossed over, and setting fire to the village, attacked the Indians in the rear. The troops under Jackson seeing the flames, and guessing the cause, at the same time made a push at the breastwork, and carried it by storm, though with the loss of some brave men. Now commenced the battle in earnest. The savages, nerved by despair, and having not the most remote idea of asking for quarter, fought desperately. Some, trying to escape across the river by swimming, were shot by the spies and mounted men under Coffee. Some took refuge among the brush and fallen timber upon the cliffs of the river from which they fired upon the victors. Jackson, desirous to save their lives, sent an interpreter within call to offer them terms, but they only fired on him, and wounded him in the shoulder. The cannon was then brought to bear on the place of their concealment, but without effect. A charge was also made, and several lives lost. And at last the brush and timber was fired, and such of them as were driven from their hiding places were shot as they ran. At length night put an end to the fight, and a few of the miserable survivors escaped in the darkness. Not over two hundred out of the whole escaped. Five hundred and fifty-seven were found dead upon the field, and three hundred women and children were captured. The loss upon the side of the Americans was fifty-five killed and 146 wounded Of these, however, nearly a third were friendly Creeks and Cherokees.

Among the Indians slain were three of their prophets, who had been most active in stirring up their country to war. Up to the last moment they maintained their influence over their deluded countrymen, and, amid the thunder of battle, painted and decorated with gaudy feathers, they continued their wild and unseemly dances and incantations. One of them, called Monohoe, while in the midst of his grotesque dancing and singing, was struck in the mouth by a grape-shot, which seems an appropriate rebuke for the impositions which he had practised on the unhappy victims that were falling around him.

After the battle of Tohopeka an incident occurred highly characteristic of the American general, and his savage foeman. An Indian about twenty years of age was brought before the General. He had received a severe wound in the leg, and a surgeon was sent for to dress it. The young savage submitted quietly to the operation, but while it was going on he looked inquiringly at the General, and said, "Cure 'im, kill 'im again?" He had no idea that there was any other doom awaiting him than that of death, and he could not comprehend why they should prepare him for death by curing his wound. The General assured him that he should not be killed, and the young Indian soon recovered. General Jackson, ascertaining that all his relations had perished in the battle, and being struck with the manly bearing of the young Indian, sent him to his own house in Tennessee. After the war he bound him out to a trade in Nashville, where he afterwards married a respectable woman of colour, and established himself in business.

THE INDIAN PRISONER.

When General Jackson left the fort at tne mouth of Cedar Creek on the Coosa River, which had been called Fort Williams, he took with him on the expedition to Tohopeka, only seven days' rations; he was therefore obliged after the battle to return again to the fort. Before leaving the scene of the battle of Tohopeka, he understood that the savages had dug up the bodies of his soldiers who had fallen at Emuckfaw and Enotochopco, for the purpose of obtaining their scalps, and exhibiting their ferocity in mutilating the lifeless bodies. The General caused his dead to be sunk in the river, and having provided every practicable comfort for his wounded, commenced his retrograde march on the 2d of April.

CHAPTER XV.

INDIAN CAMPAIGN, CONTINUED.

E have before said that the tract of country lying in the bend of the Coosa and Tallapoosa rivers, had long been considered by the Indians as consecrated ground, and that there no hostile white man's foot should ever make its track. They had been so beguiled by their prophets, who had taught them that they should there forever find security from the pale faces. It was, besides, the firm belief of the whites that the conquest of this tract of ground would soon put an end to the war.

We have seen that all the operations of the different divisions of the army were conducted with a view to a junction at the bend of these rivers. Major Floyd, with the Georgia troops, were to enter on the east side of the hostile country; Jackson with the Tennesseans on the north, while Claiborne and the Mississippians, with Williams and the United States regulars, were to make their invasion on the west and south.

The expedition planned by General Pinckney, the commander-in-chief, would all have met at this point, no doubt, as intended, had it not been for the failure of provisions to the Tennessee troops at the commencement of the campaign.

Jackson, however, after the battle of Tohopeka and his return to Fort Williams, resolved upon the complete conquest of the "Hickory Ground." He commenced preparations to attack Hoithlewalle, a town in this territory, where a considerable body of the Red-sticks were said to be concentrated. Having caused the Coosa River to be explored below Fort Williams, he saw that there was no chance of carrying his provisions by water, the roughness of the country and the poor condition of his horses, which had been so long without corn, rendering it impossible to transport them in any quantity by land: he nevertheless determined to advance with such provisions as the men could carry upon their backs, relying upon a junction with the eastern army under Colonel Milton, when their small stock should be exhausted. With this view he had requested Milton to occupy the east side of the Tallapoosa River opposite to the scene of his operations, and cut off any of the savages who might attempt to escape in that direction.

Most of the friendly Indians were dismissed, as they constituted too great a drain on his resources, and now their assistance was not deemed any longer necessary. To prepare his men for further operations, Jackson issued an animated address, in the following terms:

"Soldiers,

"You have entitled yourselves to the gratitude of your country, and your general. The expedition from which you have returned, has by your good conduct been rendered prosperous beyond any example in the history of our warfare; it has redeemed the character of your state and of that description of troops of which the greater part of you are.

"The fiends of the Tallapoosa will no longer murder our women and children, or disturb the quiet of our borders. Their midnight flambeaux will no more illumine their council-house, or shine upon the victims of their infernal orgies. In their places, a new generation will arise, who will know their duty better. The weapons of warfare will be exchanged for the utensils of husbandry; and the wilderness, which now withers in sterility and mourns the desolation which overspreads her, will blossom as the rose and become the nursery of the arts. But, before this happy day can arrive, other chastisements remain to be inflicted. It is indeed lamentable that the path to peace should lead through blood, and over the bodies of the slain; but it is a dispensation of Providence, and perhaps a wise one, to inflict partial evils that ultimate good may follow."

General Jackson commenced his march for Hoithlewalle upon the 7th of April, just five days after his return from Tohopeka. Each of his men carried upon his back eight days' provisions. It was his calculation that he would reach Hoithlewalle on the 11th; but the difficulty of travelling, owing to the heavy rains that had fallen, and which rendered the country almost impassable, prevented this.

When he reached within ten or twelve miles of Hoithlewalle, he ascertained that the town had been deserted by its inhabitants. He then directed his march for Fooshatchie, a town about three miles lower down the river, where he took several prisoners.

When the Indians of Hoithlewalle and the neighbouring towns became apprized of Jackson's ap-

proach, they precipitately fled across the Tallapoosa
River. This General Jackson had expected, and
his orders to Colonel Milton were given with a view
to prevent their escape in this direction. This
foolish officer, however, took no steps to co-operate
with him, and the consequence was, that while the
towns of Cooloome, Fooshatchie, and Hoithlewalle
were in flames, General Jackson received a letter
from him, informing him that he should cross the
Tallapoosa next day, and give the Indians battle.
Instead of the Indians being on the other side of the
Tallapoosa from that on which Milton was encamped, they had already crossed, and passed him
unmolested. A flood in the Tallapoosa and want
of provisions, prevented immediate pursuit on the
part of General Jackson, and thus the savage enemy
were suffered to escape.

General Jackson had been repeatedly informed
by General Pinckney, that 50,000 rations of flour,
and 10,000 of meat, should be furnished him by this
Colonel Milton; and the eastern army had therefore
placed full reliance on this, and expected to receive
supplies from him as soon as he could form a
junction. On application, however, to Colonel Milton, that officer replied that he did not feel himself
under any obligation to supply the Tennessee troops.

but would the next day lend them a small supply of provisions. Milton had crossed the Tallapoosa, and was advancing to attack Hoithlewalle, which was already in ashes. Jackson, being informed of his position and movements, sent him a peremptory order, by Captain Gordon of the spies, requiring him to furnish the provisions which he had previously requested, and to form a junction with him the next day. On reading the order, Colonel Milton inquired of Captain Gordon, what sort of a man General Jackson was.

"He is a man," replied the captain, "who intends when he gives an order that it shall be obeyed."

Colonel Milton said he would furnish the provisions, not because they were ordered, but because the men were suffering for want of them:—but he nevertheless obeyed the order, and formed the junction as required.

Jackson, in order to intercept the enemy who had fled, despatched a body of mounted men to scour the left bank of the Tallapoosa River, while he himself, with the main army, prepared to march down the Coosa as far as their junction. In the morning, just as the army was about to commence its march, word was brought to General Jackson, that Colonel Milton's brigade could not move, as the wagon-horses had strayed away in the nigh and could not be found. Jackson sent back word to Milton, that he had discovered in such cases, a very effectual remedy, and that if he would detail twenty men to each wagon the difficulty would be overcome. Milton took the hint, and having dismounted a few of his dragoons, and using their horses, the wagons were soon in motion.

Not the least opposition did the army experience in their march from the Indians, and it had now become apparent that the battle of Tohcpeka had ended the Creek war.

No effort to rally, after that fatal day, had been made by the surviving warriors, and as General Jackson advanced, they either fled before him or came in and offered submission. The first to submit were the chiefs of the Hickory Ground, and as soon as it was known, all through the territory, that their lives would be spared, a general submission was the consequence, so that in a short time after this the Indian campaign was put to an end, and the Tennessee army returned home to their own state, and **were** honourably discharged.

CHAPTER XVI.

SOUTHERN CAMPAIGN AGAINST THE BRITISH.

JACKSON was now (spring of 1814,) appointed to be a major-general in the service of the United States. The protection of the coast near the mouths of the Mississippi was intrusted to him; and his first attention was turned to the comfort, the encouragement, the protection which the savages received from the Spanish governor and Spanish authorities in the fortress of Pensacola, which is situated on the Gulf of Mexico, at about a hundred miles' distance from New Orleans, about thirty miles from the frontiers of the state of Alabama, and about a hundred miles from the main fastness of the Creek Indians. His opinion was, that the savages were always receiving assistance from the Spanish garrison, and from the British, through the means of that garrison; and he was persuaded that, finally, the British would assail

New Orleans by means of preparations made at Pensacola. On his way to the south, he learned that about three hundred British troops had landed, and were fortifying themselves at no great distance from Pensacola. In this state of things, he endeavoured to prevail upon the Spanish governor to desist from all acts injurious to the United States. But that officer was by no means inclined to truth or sincerity. He falsified and prevaricated. By this time, and indeed before this time, the news had been received of the fall of Napoleon and his banishment to Elba. This event had greatly increased the means of Great Britain for hostile operations against the United States. This Spanish garrison was, in fact, a rendezvous for the British : it was a rendezvous for the savage enemies of the United States. Captain Gordon, sent by Jackson to see what was passing, in the month of August (1814), reported to the General that he had seen from fifty to two hundred officers and soldiers, a park of artillery, about five hundred savages under the drill of British officers, and dressed in the English uniform.

Apprised of these doings, General Jackson resolved at once to march to Pensacola, and put an end to this duplicity on the part of the Spanish governor of that place.

Colonel Nicholls, at the head of a British expedition, had issued a proclamation, dated from his "head-quarters at Pensacola," leaving no farther doubt of the treachery of the Spanish government.

The first act of hostility on the part of the British, was an assault upon Fort Bowyer, a post of the United States on the Mobile. On the 15th of September, 1814, Nicholls attacked the fort by land, while several vessels, mounting altogether about ninety guns, approached by sea. The expedition ended by the blowing up of one of the English ships, greatly damaging another, and sending off Colonel Nicholls, the proclamation-maker, with the loss of one of his ships, and, as it was said, one of his eyes.

The commander of Fort Bowyer was a Major Lawrence. His brave band consisted of about one hundred and fifty men, while the force of the British was, as we have seen, ninety guns by sea, while Nicholls assaulted the fort by land, with a twelve pound howitzer, and several hundreds of marines, sailors, and savages. This affair was in the highest degree honourable to Major Lawrence and his men. The disparity of force was immense; and the defeat of the British, in this their first demonstration, must have had a material influence on subsequent operations

G

Jackson was a man, however, who did not stop with half-way measures, and he was in this case determined to carry out his plans, and break up the rendezvous at Pensacola. Accordingly, on the 6th of November, 1814, he marched against it, demolished all its defences and protections, drove out the British and the savages, and demonstrated that there was enough American energy to put down any triple combination of English, Spaniards and savages.

Having given the haughty and insolent foe a foretaste of that which was to come, he repaired to the point which was to be the grand scene of action He arrived at the city of New Orleans on the 1st of December, 1814. News had been received of the approach of a British fleet. The first intelligence of this sort was received on the 4th of December. Cochrane, who commanded the British fleet, and who had the celebrated Sir George Cockburn under him, had collected all their forces together, after they had been beaten off from before Baltimore, and had sailed for New Orleans, whither Nicholls had been sent before to prepare the way for the proclamation, which had just been issued from his head-quarters at Pensacola. They were to be joined, as they afterwards were, by a strong body of the " heroes of the Peninsula." Their force altogether was prodigious : ships of the line, frigates, sloops of war, fire-ships, great numbers of furnaces to heat red-hot shot, Congreve rockets, all manner of materials for sapping, and mining, and blowing up : an expedition costing, in all probability, more than a million of pounds sterling in the fitting out. There were eleven thousand regular " heroes of the Peninsula ;" there were four generals, two admirals, twelve thousand, at the least, of seamen and marines, artillery in abundance, of all sorts ; perhaps a hundred gun-boats and barges ; and every expense ready to be incurred for the employment of persons of all sorts ; besides numerous bands of savages ready to come in, if the attack had succeeded.

Such was the mighty armament prepared for the conquest of New Orleans. But the city had a defender whose energy, skill, and promptness, eminently fitted him for the perilous task of opposing these great forces.

CHAPTER XVII.

JACKSON AT NEW ORLEANS.

E have seen that Jackson, having received intelligence which made him believe, and quite certain indeed, that the intention of the British was to get possession of the mouths of the Mississippi, of the whole state of Louisiana, and particularly of that rich prize, the city of New Orleans, crammed with sugar, coffee, flour, cotton, and all sorts of merchandise, repaired thither, that is to say, to the city itself, on the 1st of December, 1814. On the 6th of December, he received certain intelligence that a large British force was off the port of Pensacola, destined against New Orleans; that it amounted to about eighty vessels, and that more than double that number were momentarily looked for to form a junction with those already arrived; that there were in this fleet vessels of all descriptions, contrived for the most deadly purposes, with a large body of land troops; that Admiral Cochrane had the command, and that his ship, the Tonnant, was then lying off Pensacola.

It must here be observed, that the city of New Orleans, at this time containing a population of about 30,000 inhabitants, had been purchased from the French only three years before, (in 1811,) and that most of its citizens were of Spanish and French descent. From this it will easily be understood that their attachment to their new government was anything but warm, and in fact the greater number of these people, having been educated and brought up in the monarchical countries of Europe, would have preferred that the British should have taken the city, provided they had been left unmolested. When this is taken into account, it will easily be imagined that General Jackson, in preparing to defend it, had other difficulties to contend against, than mere want of troops, ammunition, and arms. He had something else than mere fighting to do: he had to contend against treason in every quarter and corner, and treason on the part of those whose very hearths and homes and lives he had come to defend from a ruthless and mercenary soldiery. He was obliged, as will easily be supposed, to place the city under

martial law, and in one instance, where he had
ordered a traitor to be imprisoned, and where that
traitor had been set at liberty by Judge Hall, the
General thought it necessary to imprison the judge
also.   These, to be sure, seem harsh measures, but
the necessity of the case required harsh measures,
and had such measures not have been taken, New
Orleans would, most undoubtedly, have fallen into
the hands of the British, and our country would have
suffered incalculable disgrace and disaster.   In the
midst of every kind of difficulty, with his faithful
little army, did General Jackson await the British
invader.   He had, to be sure, a faithful army, with
faithful officers; but they were badly armed and
equipped, while the citizens around him had almost
yielded to despair, thinking that, with such means,
there was not the slightest hope of opposing the
splendid armament that was coming against them,
and which consisted of the flower of the British
army who had just conquered Napoleon Bonaparte.

It was with these difficulties and dangers staring
him in the face, that General Jackson proceeded to
make preparations to surmount them all, and the
manner in which he succeeded will be related in the
following chapters.

CHAPTER XVIII.

BATTLE OF THE TWENTY-THIRD OF DECEMBER.

N order that the reader may the more fully understand the military operations carried on in the defence of New Orleans, it may not be improper to make a few remarks upon the peculiar situation of that city.

New Orleans is about one hundred and five miles from the mouths of the Mississippi River, and situated around a bend, on the left, or eastern bank. It is generally approached by vessels by the river, although small craft, such as schooners and sloops, navigate lakes Pontchartrain and Borgne (an arm of the sea, lying behind the city, and separated from it, as well as from the river, by a narrow tract of country, which is, for the most part, an impassable and forest-covered swamp.) A narrow strip of land, varying from a few hundred yards to two or three miles, borders the river, gradually tapering off into a swamp as it recedes, until it reaches the lakes. This strip of land is covered with plantations of sugar and cotton, &c., and protected from inundations of the river by an embankment of earth, called the "Levee," which runs up far above the city. The same is found on both sides of the river.

Now the English armament, instead of coming up the river, entered the lakes and commenced landing their forces, on the 23d of December, upon this strip of dry land, about eight miles below the city. They reached the dry land by means of a stream or "Bayou," (a sort of natural canal,) called the Bayou Bienvenu, through which they passed in their boats. They were as yet ignorant that Jackson had been making such preparations to receive them, and instead of marching directly upon the city, which would have been the safest course, their commander resolved to encamp where he had landed, on the plantations of two or three French settlers.

When General Jackson received intelligence that the British were landing through Bienvenu and Villere's canal, he determined to attack them instantly, and therefore ordered the brigades of generals Coffee and Carroll, who were encamped about four miles above New Orleans, into the city. So prompt were these, that in two hours they were in the streets and ready. As yet General Jackson could not tell what force of the British had arrived at Lacoste's and Laronde's plantations, (these were the plantations lying between the river and tho Bayou Bienvenu,) nor whether this was not in-tended as a feint to draw off his attention from some other point of approach, for, as we have seen, there were several other directions by which tho city might be reached. Labouring under this doubt, he detached General Carroll with his division, along with Governor Claiborne and the Louisiana militia, to take post on the Gentilly road, which led from Chef Menteur (another landing-place,) to New Or-leans. Their orders were to defend this approach should the British make their appearance on it, to the last extremity.

With the remainder of his troops, in all about 2000 men, Jackson hastened down the river towards the point where it had been reported the British were effecting a landing.

Alarm pervaded the city. The marching and countermarching of the troops, the proximity of the enemy, with the approaching contest, and uncer-tainty of the issue, had excited a general fear. Already might the British be on their way and at hand before the necessary arrangements could be made to oppose them. To prevent this, Colonel Hayne, with two companies of riflemen and the Mississippi dragoons, was sent forward to reconnoitre their camp, learn their position and their numbers, and if they should be found advancing, to harass and oppose them at every step until the main body should arrive.

Everything being ready, General Jackson commenced his march, to meet and fight the veteran troops of England. An inconsiderable circumstance at this moment evinced what unlimited confidence was reposed in his skill and bravery. As his troops were marching through the city, his ears were assailed with the screams and cries of innumerable females, who had collected on the way, and seemed to apprehend the worst of consequences. Feeling for their distresses, and anxious to quiet them, he directed Mr. Livingston, one of his aids-de-camp, to address them in the French language. "Say to them," said he, "not to be alarmed: the enemy shall never reach the city." It operated like an electric shock upon these terrified creatures. To know that he, himself, was not afraid of a fatal result, inspired them at once with confidence, and changed their fears into hopes.

The General arrived within sight of the enemy's position a little before dark, and having previously gotten from a colonel, who had been sent in advance, some tolerable idea of their strength, (he thought it was about 2000 : it proved, however, to be 3000, as was afterwards found, and was constantly increasing by reinforcements from the vessels,) he determined upon an immediate attack. It was planned in the following manner : Coffee, with one division of the army, was to march to the left, keeping near the swamp, and thus, if possible, turn the enemy's right, and drive them toward the river, where a schooner-of-war, (the Caroline,) commanded by Commodore Patterson, would drop down and open upon them. The main division of Jackson's army, led by himself, would advance down the main road, near the river, and attack the fresh landed troops in front.

These plans being arranged, they were immediately entered upon.

General Coffee with silence and caution had advanced beyond their pickets, next the swamp, and nearly reached the point to which he was ordered, when a broadside from the Caroline announced the battle begun. Patterson had proceeded slowly, giving time, as he believed, for the execution of those arrangements contemplated on the shore. So sanguine had the British been in the belief that they would be kindly received, and little opposition attempted, that the Caroline floated by the sentinels, and anchored before their camp without any kind of molestation. On passing the front picket she was hailed in a low tone of voice, but not returning an answer, no further question was made. This, added to some other attendant circumstances, confirmed the opinion that they believed her a vessel laden with provisions, which had been sent out from New Orleans, and was intended for them. Having reached what, from their fires, appeared to be the centre of their encampment, her anchors were cast, and her character and business disclosed from her guns. So unexpected an attack produced a momentary confusion; but recovering, she was answered by a discharge of musketry and flight of Congreve rockets, which passed without injury, while the grape and canister from her guns were pouring destructively on them. To take away the certainty of aim afforded by the light from their fires, these were immediately extinguished, and they retired two or three hundred yards into the open field, if not out of the reach of cannon, at least to a distance, where by the darkness of the n.ght they would be protected.

Coffee had dismounted his men, and turned his horses loose, at a large ditch, next the swamp, in the rear of Laronde's plantation, and gained, as he thought, the centre of the enemy's line, when the signal from the Caroline reached him. He directly wheeled his column in, and forming, marched toward the river and the enemy. He had not proceeded more than an hundred yards, when he received a heavy fire from the enemy's line formed in front. This he did not expect, as he supposed they were much nearer the bank of the river, and so they had been, until the fire of the Caroline drove them nearer the swamp, and consequently nearer to Coffee. The moon was shining, but so feebly that it was difficult to distinguish objects at any distance. As Coffee's forces were mostly riflemen, orders were given them not to fire at random, but to make certain shots. Going on for some time with caution, they at last came in sight of the enemy, when a general discharge of the American rifles caused them to retreat; they, however, rallied again, and formed, when they were again attacked and again forced to retreat.

The brave yeomanry, led on by their gallant commander, pressed fearlessly forward, driving their

assailants from every position which they took up
Their general was under no necessity to encourage
them by words; his own example was sufficient to
excite them.   Always in the midst, he displayed a
coolness and disregard of danger, calling to his
troops that they had often said they could fight—
now was the time to prove it.

The British, driven back by the resolute firmness
and ardour of the assailants, had now reached a
grove of orange-trees, with a ditch running past it,
protected by a fence on the margin.   Here they
were halted and formed for battle.   It was a favourable position, promising security, and was occupied
with a confidence that they could not be forced to
yield it. Coffee's dauntless yeomanry, strengthened in
their hopes of success, moved on, nor discovered the
advantages against them, until a fire from the entire
British line showed their position and defence.   A
sudden check was given ; but it was only momentary,
for gathering fresh ardour, they charged across the
ditch, gave a deadly and destructive fire, and forced
the enemy once more to give way.   The retreat
continued, until gaining a similar position, the British
made another stand, and were again driven from it
with considerable loss.

Thus the battle raged on the left wing, until the

British reached the bank of the river; here a deter
mined stand was made, and further encroachments
resisted: for half an hour the conflict was extremely
violent on both sides. The American troops could
not be driven from their purpose, nor the British
made to yield their ground; but at length, having
suffered greatly, the latter were under the necessity
of taking refuge behind the levee, which afforded a
breastwork, and protected them from the fatal fire
of our riflemen. Coffee, unacquainted with their
position, for the darkness had greatly increased,
already contemplated again to charge them; but
one of his officers, who had discovered the advantage their situation gave them, assured him it was
too hazardous; that they could be driven no farther,
and would, from the point they occupied, resist with
the bayonet, and repel, with considerable loss, any
attempt that might be made to dislodge them. The
place of their retirement was covered in front by a
strong bank, which had been extended into the field.
to keep out the river, in consequence of the first
being encroached upon, and undermined in several
places: the former, however, was still entire in
many parts, which, interposing between them and
the Mississippi, afforded security from the broad-
sides of the schooner, which lay off at some distance.

A further apprehension, lest. by moving still neare.
to the river, he might greatly expose himself to the
fire of the Caroline, which was yet spiritedly main
taining the conflict, induced Coffee to retire until he
could hear from the commanding general, and receive his further orders.

While General Coffee was thus employed upon
the left, and next the swamp, the main division
under Jackson had been led down the Levee road.
Instead of moving in column, which had been ordered by Jackson, and which order had been omitted
to be executed, the troops had been formed in line,
and thus commenced their march, but although the
ground was wide enough for this, at first, it gradually
grew narrower, and the centre became compressed,
and was forced into the rear. The river gradually
inclining to the left, diminished the space, and Laronde's house, surrounded by a grove of clustered
orange trees, compressed the left wing, so that two
battalions (Planche's and Daquin's,) were thrown
into confusion. This could have been easily re-
medied, but for the briskness of the advance, and
the darkness of the night. A heavy fire from behind
a fence, immediately before them, had brought the
enemy to view. Acting in obedience to their orders,
not to waste their ammunition at random, our troops

had pressed forward against the opposition in their front, and thereby threw those battalions in the rear

A fog rising from the river, and which, added to the smoke from the guns, was covering the plain, gradually diminished the little light shed by the moon, and greatly increased the darkness of the night : no clue was left to ascertain how or where the enemy were situated. There was no alternative but to move on in the direction of their fire, which subjected the assailants to material disadvantages. The British, driven from their first position, had retired back, and occupied another, behind a deep ditch, that ran out of the Mississippi towards the swamp, on the margin of which was a wood-railed fence. Here, strengthened by increased numbers, they again opposed the advance of our troops. Having waited until they had approached sufficiently near to be discovered, from their fastnesses they discharged a fire upon the advancing army. Instantly our battery was formed, and poured destructively upon them; while the infantry, pressing forward, aided in the conflict, which at this point was for some time spiritedly maintained. At this moment a brisk sally was made upon our advance, when the marines, unequal to the assault, were already giving way. The adjutant-general, and Colonels Piatt and

H

Chotard, with a part of the seventh, hastening to their support, drove the enemy, and saved the artillery from capture. General Jackson, perceiving the decided advantages which were derived from the position they occupied, ordered their line to be charged. It was obeyed with cheerfulness, and executed with promptness. Pressing on, our troops gained the ditch, and pouring across it a well-aimed fire, compelled them to retreat, and to abandon their intrenchment. The plain on which they were contending was cut to pieces by races from the river to convey the water to the swamp. The enemy were therefore very soon enabled to occupy another position, equally favourable with the one whence they had been just driven, where they formed for battle, and for some time gallantly maintained themselves; but which at length, and after stubborn resistance, they were forced to yield.

The enemy, discovering the firm and obstinate advance made by the right wing of the American army, and presuming, perhaps, that its principal strength was posted on the road, formed the intention of attacking violently the left. Obliquing for this purpose, an attempt was made to turn it. At this moment, Daquin's and the battalion of city

guards, being marched up and formed on the left of
the forty-fourth regiment, met and repulsed them.

The darkness of the night prevented the advantages which might have been obtained by our artillery; nevertheless, guided by the blaze of the enemy's
musquetry, it had been used with such effect as
greatly to annoy them.

The enemy had been thrice assailed and beaten,
and had been forced for nearly a mile down the
river. They had now retired so that they were
only to be found amidst the darkness of night. The
General, therefore, before proceeding farther, resolved to halt until he could ascertain what had
been the result of Coffee's attack on the enemy's
right. He knew from the brisk firing he had heard
in that direction, that he had been warmly engaged,
but as that had nearly ceased, as well as the firing
from the Caroline, he thought proper to halt, and
ascertain what had been his success. Having
earned, therefore, that from the darkness some confusion had been produced in Coffee's ranks, similar
to that which had arisen in his own, he determined
to prosecute the battle no farther, but wait until the
morning light should enable him to discover the
position of his enemy.

It had been Jackson's belief that he might be

enabled to capture the whole British army, by fol
lowing up his success, and from the fact that they
having just landed, and being entirely ignorant of
the nature of the country or of the strength of their
opponents, there was sufficient reason upon which
to ground this belief: but when Jackson heard from
Coffee of the strong position into which the enemy
had been driven, and also that a division of his
(Coffee's,) troops had been detached, and were
probably captured, he ordered the army back to the
original position.

The party that had been detached from General
Coffee's command, were colonels Dyer and Gibson,
with about two hundred men, and Captain Beal's
company of riflemen.

Dyer, who commanded the extreme left, on clear-
ing a grove after the enemy had retired, was
marching in a direction where he expected to find
General Coffee; he very soon discovered a force in
front, and halting his men, hastened towards it;
arriving within a short distance, he was hailed,
ordered to stop, and report to whom he belonged:
Dyer, and Gibson, his lieutenant-colonel, who had
accompanied him, advanced and stated they were of
Coffee's brigade; by this time they had arrived
within a short distance of the line, and perceiving

that the name of the brigade they had stated was
not understood, their apprehensions were awakened
lest it might be a detachment of the enemy; in this
opinion they were confirmed, and wheeling to return,
were fired on and pursued. Gibson had scarcely
started when he fell; before he could recover, a
soldier quicker than the rest had reached him, and
pinned him to the ground with his bayonet; fortunately the stab had but slightly wounded him,
and he was only held by his clothes; thus pinioned,
and perceiving others to be briskly advancing, but a
moment was left for deliberation; making a violent
exertion, and springing to his feet, he threw his
assailant to the ground, and made good his escape.
Colonel Dyer had retreated about fifty yards, when
his horse dropped dead; entangled in the fall, and
slightly wounded in the thigh, there was little
prospect of relief, for the enemy were briskly advancing; his men being near at hand, he ordered
them to advance and fire, which checked their approach, and enabled him to escape. Being now at
the head of his command,—perceiving an enemy in
a direction he had not expected, and uncertain how
or where he might find General Coffee, he determined to seek him to the right, and moving on with
his little band, forced his way through the enemy's

lines, with the loss of sixty-three of his men, who were killed and taken. Captain Beal, with equal bravery, charged through the enemy, carrying off some prisoners, and losing several of his own company.

The battle of the 23d was well planned, and but for the confusion introduced into the ranks, and the Caroline having given her signals too early, before Coffee had made his arrangements on the side toward the swamp, it would have been attended with complete success. The battle, however, of the night of the 23d, was of the utmost importance in its results, as it had the effect of checking the enemy in their advance toward the city, which would have doubtless been attempted next day. By this, as we shall presently see, Jackson obtained time to complete that impregnable and ever-memorable fortification, by the assistance of which, he was enabled to repel an army of twice his own numbers, and defend a wealthy city from pillage and ruin.

CHAPTER XIX.

FURTHER OPERATIONS

ACKSON having now ascertained that the enemy were making their principal landing through the Bayou Bienvenu, immediately despatched orders for General Carroll to join him with the troops, which, it will be recollected, had been left to defend the approach by Chef Menteur.

Ascertaining, moreover, that about 6000 of the enemy were already on the ground, he saw that his best course would be to occupy some fortified position, and act upon the defensive until he could discover the future views of the enemy, and until he should receive expected reinforcements from Kentucky.

Pursuing this idea, at four o'clock in the morning, having ordered Colonel Hinds to occupy the ground he was then abandoning, and to observe the enemy closely, he fell back, and formed his line behind a

deep ditch, that stretched to the swamp at right
angles from the river. There were two circumstances strongly recommending the importance of
this place :—the swamp, which from the highlands
at Baton Rouge skirts the river at irregular dis-
tances, and in many places is almost impervious,
had here approached within four hundred yards of
the Mississippi, and hence, from the narrowness of
the pass, was more easily to be defended ; added to
which, there was a deep canal, whence the dirt being
thrown on the upper side, already formed a tolerable
work of defence.   Behind this his troops were
formed, and proper measures adopted for increasing
its strength, with a determination never to abandon
it ; but there to resist to the last, and valiantly to
defend those rights which were sought to be out-
raged and destroyed.

Promptitude and decision, and activity in execution, constituted the leading traits of Jackson's
character. No sooner had he resolved on the course
which he thought necessary to be pursued, than with
every possible despatch he hastened to its completion. Before him was an army proud of its name,
and distinguished for its deeds of valour ; opposed
to which was his own unbending spirit, and an in-
ferior, undisciplined, and unarmed force. He con-

ceived, therefore, that his was a defensive policy that by prudence and caution he would be able to preserve what offensive operation might have a tendency to endanger. Hence, with activity and industry, based on a hope of ultimate success, he commenced his plan of defence, determining to fortify himself as effectually as the peril and pressure of the moment would permit. When to expect attack he could not tell; preparation and readiness to meet it was for him to determine on, all else was for the enemy. Promptly, therefore, he proceeded with his system of defence; and with such thoughtfulness and anxiety, that until the night of the 27th, when his line was completed, he never slept, or for a moment closed his eyes. Resting his hope of safety here, he was everywhere, through the night, present, encouraging his troops and hastening a completion of the work. For five days and four nights he was without sleep, and constantly employed. His line of defence (the celebrated cotton embankment,) being completed, on the night of the 27th he, for the first time since the arrival of the enemy, retired to rest and repose.

From the violence of the assault already made, the fears of the British had been greatly excited; to keep their apprehensions alive was considered important, with a view partially to destroy the overweening confidence with which they had arrived on our shores, and to compel them to act for a time upon the defensive. To effect this, General Coffee, with his brigade, was ordered down on the morning of the 24th, to unite with Colonel Hinds, and make a show in the rear of Lacoste's plantation. The enemy, not yet recovered from the panic produced by the assault of the preceding evening, already believed it was in contemplation to urge another attack, and immediately formed themselves to repel it; but Coffee, having succeeded in recovering some of his horses, which were wandering along the margin of the swamp, and in regaining part of the clothing which his troops had lost the night before, returned to the line, leaving them to conjecture the objects of his movement.

Besides the line of defence which Jackson was forming on the left bank of the river, he also had prepared defences at other points where he thought he enemy might approach.

Major Reynolds had been despatched to fortify the bayous leading from Barrataria, in company with Lafitte, who, from his lively zeal in favour of his adopted country, had been pardoned by the United States, and received into their service. Chef

Menteur was also defended by Major Lacoste, and the fortifications on the right bank of the Mississippi were under the direction of Morgan. He feared that the shipping of the enemy might come up the river, and therefore forts St. Philip and Bourbon were put in the best order to prevent this.

On the 27th the enemy opened a battery (which they had erected for the purpose,) upon the schooner Caroline. She, it will be recollected, on the night of the 23d had dropped down opposite the enemy's lines, and it had been impossible since to warp her up again, and although she could easily have been carried down the river until under the protection of one of the forts, yet it had been thought better to keep her where she lay, (on the opposite side of the river,) and wait the chances of a favourable wind to carry her up.

The enemy, however, succeeded in lodging a red-hot shot in her hold, which set her on fire, and she being abandoned, shortly after blew up.

Gathering confidence from the destruction of the Caroline, on the morning of the 28th the enemy (now increased in numbers and commanded in person by Major-General Sir Edward Packenham,) advanced to storm our works. They were, however, defeated in the engagement, with the loss of over one hundred killed, while the loss upon our side was only eight or ten.

A supposed disaffection in New Orleans, and an enemy in front, were circumstances well calculated to excite unpleasant forebodings. General Jackson believed it necessary and essential to his security, while contending with avowed foes, not to be wholly nattentive to danger lurking at home; but by guarding vigilantly, to be able to suppress any treasonable purpose the moment it should be developed, and it should have time to mature. Treason to their country, however, first made its appearance in the very place where it should have been last in showing itself—in the halls of the legislature.

Jackson, hearing that this body were contemplating to surrender the city in case of an emergency, ordered Governor Claiborne to shut them up in the hall, so that their deliberations should not affect the people ; but Claiborne, mistaking the order, instead of shutting them up turned them out, and thus practically dissolved that body.

Before this he had been called on by a special committee of the legislature to know what his course would be should necessity force him from his position. " If," replied the General, " I thought the hair of my head could divine what I should do

forthwith, I would cut it off; go back with this
answer; say to your honourable body, that if disaster does overtake me, and the fate of war drives
me from my line to the city, they may expect to have
a very warm session."—"And what did you design
to do," I inquired, "provided you had been forced
to retreat?"—"I should," he replied, "have retreated
to the city, fired it, and fought the enemy amid the
surrounding flames. There were with me men of
wealth, owners of considerable property, who, in
such an event, would have been among the foremost
to have applied the torch to their own buildings;
and what they had left undone I should have completed. Nothing for the comfortable maintenance
of the enemy would have been left in the rear. I
would have destroyed New Orleans—occupied a
position above on the river—cut off all supplies, and
in this way compelled them to depart from the
country."

The British admiral on the lakes, solicitous to
ascertain the number and position of Jackson's
army, resorted to various means to obtain this information from two gentlemen, Mr. Shields and
Doctor Murrell, who (although bearing a flag of
truce,) had been taken prisoners on the 14th.

Shields was perceived to be quite deaf, and calculating on some advantage to be derived from this circumstance, he and the Doctor were placed at night in the green-room, where any conversation which occurred between them could readily be heard. Suspecting, perhaps, something of the kind, after having retired, and everything was seemingly still, they began to speak of their situation—the circumstance of their being detained, and of the prudent caution with which they had guarded themselves against communicating any information to the British admiral. But, continued Shields, how greatly these gentlemen will be disappointed in their expectations, for Jackson, with the twenty thousand troops he now has, and the reinforcements from Kentucky, which must speedily reach him, will be able to destroy any force that can be landed from these ships. Every word was heard and treasured, and not supposing there was any design, or that he presumed himself overheard, they were beguiled by it, and at once concluded our force to be as great as it was represented; and hence, 'no doubt, arose the reason of that prudent care and caution with which the enemy afterward proceeded; for "nothing," remarked a British officer, at the close of the invasion, "was kept a secret from us except your numbers; this, although diligently sought after could never be procured."

Every precaution was adopted to prevent any communication by which the slightest intelligence should be had of our situation, already indeed sufficiently deplorable. Additional guards were posted along the swamp, on both sides of the Mississippi, to arrest all intercourse; while on the river, the common highway, watch-boats were constantly plying during the night, in different directions, so that a log could scarcely float down the stream unperceived. Two flat-bottomed boats, on a dark night, were turned adrift above, to ascertain if vigilance were preserved, and whether there would be any possibility of escaping the guards and passing in safety to the British lines. The light boats discovered them on their passage, and on the alarm being given, they were opened upon by the Louisiana sloop, and the batteries on the shore, and in a few minutes were sunk. In spite, however, of every precaution, treason still discovered avenues through which to project and execute her nefarious plans, and through them was constantly afforded information to the enemy; carried to them, no doubt, by adventurous friends, who sought and effected their nightly passage through the deepest parts of the swamp, where it was impossible for sentinels to be stationed.

Frequent light skirmishes by advanced parties, without material effect on either side, were the only incidents that took place for several days. .

Upon the morning of the 1st of January, however, the enemy, who for three days had been engaged in erecting batteries, made another attack upon our fortifications. They were obliged, however, to retire, and their batteries having failed to make a breach, were silenced and rendered useless by the American cannon. The enemy in this affair lost about seventy men, while our loss was only eleven killed.

The enemy's heavy shot having penetrated our intrenchment in many places, it was discovered not to be as strong as had at first been imagined. Fatigue parties were again employed, and its strength daily increased: an additional number of bales of cotton were taken to be applied to strengthening and defending the embrasures along the line. A Frenchman, whose property had been thus, without his consent, seized, fearful of the injury it might sustain, proceeded in person to General Jackson to reclaim it, and to demand its delivery. The General, having heard his complaint, and ascertained from him that he was unemployed in any military service, directed a musket to be brought to him, and placing it in his hand, ordered him on the line, remarking, at the same time, that as he seemed to be a man possessed of property, he knew of none who had a better right to fight and to defend it.

CHAPTER XX.

N the 4th of this month, the long expected reinforcement from Kentucky, amounting to 2250 men, under the command of Major-general Thomas, arrived at head-quarters; but so ill provided with arms as to be incapable of rendering any considerable service.

Information was now received that Major-general Lambert had joined the British commander-in-chief with a considerable reinforcement. It had been heretofore announced in the American camp that additional forces were expected, and something decisive might be looked for as soon as they should arrive. This circumstance, in connexion with others no less favouring the idea, had led to the conclusion that a few days more would, in all probability, bring on the struggle which would decide the fate of the city. It was more than ever necessary to keep

concealed the situation of his army ; and, above all,
to preserve as secret as possible its unarmed condition. To restrict all communication even with his
own lines, was now, as danger increased, rendered
more important. None were permitted to leave the
line, and none from without to pass into his camp.
but such as were to be implicitly confided in." The
line of sentinels was strengthened in front, that
none might pass to the enemy, should desertion be
attempted : yet, notwithstanding this precaution and
care, his plans and situation were disclosed. On
the night of the 6th of January, a soldier from the
line by some means succeeded in eluding the vigilance of our sentinels. Early next morning his
departure was discovered : it was at once correctly
conjectured he had gone over to the enemy, and
would, no doubt, afford them all the information in
his power to communicate. This opinion, as subsequent circumstances disclosed, was well founded :
and dearly did he atone for his crime. He unfolded
to the British the situation of the American line, the
late reinforcements we had received, and the unarmed condition of many of the troops ; and pointing
to the centre of General Carroll's division, as a place
occupied by militia alone. recommended it as the

point where an attack might be most prudently and
safely made.

Everything was in readiness to meet the assault
when it should be made. The redoubt on the levee
was defended by a company of the seventh regiment,
under the command of Lieutenant Ross. The
regular troops occupied that part of the intrenchment next the river. General Carroll's division was
in the centre, supported by the Kentucky troops,
under General John Adair; while the extreme left,
extending for a considerable distance into the swamp,
was protected by the brigade of General Coffee.
How soon the attack would be waged, was uncertain; at what moment rested with the enemy,—
with us, to be in readiness for resistance. There
were many circumstances, however, favouring the
belief that the hour of contest was not far distant,
and indeed fast approaching; the bustle of to-day,
—the efforts to carry their boats into the river,—
the fascines and scaling-ladders that were preparing,
were circumstances pointing to attack, and indicat-
ing the hour to be near at hand. General Jackson,
unmoved by appearances, anxiously desired a contest which he believed would give a triumph to his
arms, and terminate the hardships of his suffering
soldiers. Unremitting in exertion, and constantly

vigilant, his precaution kept pace with the zeal and preparation of the enemy. He seldom slept: he was always at his post per rming the duties both of general and soldier. His sentinels were doubled, and extended as far as possible in the direction of the British camp; while a considerable portion of the troops were constantly at the line, with arms in their hands, ready to act when the first alarm should be given.

For eight days had the two armies lain upon the same field within sight of each other, without anything decisive having been effected. The 8th of January at length arrived. The day dawned, and the signals intended to produce concert in the enemy's movements were descried. On the left, near the swamp, a skyrocket was perceived rising in the air—it was answered by another on the right: instantly the enemy's charge was made, and with such rapidity that our outposts had hardly time to reach the lines. The British batteries opened with showers of bombs and shells, while the air was blazing with their congreve rockets.

The two divisions, commanded by Sir Edward Packenham in person, and supported by generals Keane and Gibbs, pressed forward; the right against the centre of General Carroll's command, the left against our redoubt on the levee. A thick fog that obscured the morning enabled them to approach within a short distance of our intrenchment before they were discovered. They were now perceived advancing with a firm, quick, and steady pace, in column, with a front of sixty or seventy deep. Our troops, who had for some time been in readiness, and waiting their appearance, gave three cheers, and instantly the whole line was lighted with the blaze of their fire. A burst of artillery and small arms, pouring with destructive aim upon them, mowed down their front, and arrested their advance. In our musketry there was not a moment's intermission: as one party discharged their pieces, another succeeded; alternately loading and appearing, no pause could be perceived—it was one continued volley. The columns already perceived their dangerous and exposed situation. Battery No. 7, on the left, was ably served by Lieutenant Spotts, and galled them with an incessant and destructive fire Batteries No. 6 and 8 were no less actively employed, and no less successful in felling them to the ground. Notwithstanding the severity of our fire, which few troops could for a moment have withstood, some of those brave men pressed on, and succeeded in gaining the ditch in front of our works, where they remained during the action, and were afterward made prisoners. The horror before them was too great to be withstood: and already were the British troops seen wavering in their determination, and receding from the conflict. At this moment, Sir Edward Packenham, hastening to the front, endeavoured to encourage and inspire them with renewed zeal. His example was of short continuance: he soon fell mortally wounded in the arms of his aid-de-camp, not far from our line. Generals Gibbs and Keane also fell, and were borne from the field dangerously wounded. At this moment, General Lambert, who was advancing at a small distance in the rear, with the reserve, met the columns precipitately retreating, and in great confusion. His efforts to stop them were unavailing, they continued retreating until they reached a ditch at the distance of four hundred yards, where a momentary safety being found, they were rallied and halted.

The field before them, over which they had advanced, was strewed with the dead and dying. Danger hovered still around; yet urged and encouraged by their officers, who feared their own disgrace involved in the failure, they again moved to the charge. They were already near enough to deploy, and were endeavouring to do so; but the same constant and unremitted resistance that caused their first retreat, continued yet unabated. Our batteries had never ceased their fire; their constant discharges of grape and canister, and the fatal aim of our musketry, mowed down the front of the columns as fast as they could be formed. Satisfied nothing could be done, and that certain destruction awaited all further attempts, they forsook the contest and the field in disorder, leaving it almost entirely covered with the dead and wounded. It was in vain their officers endeavoured to animate them to further efforts, and equally vain to attempt coercion. The panic produced from the dreadful repulse they had experienced, the plain on which they had acted being covered with innumerable bodies of their country-men, while with their most zealous exertions they had been unable to obtain the slightest advantage, were circumstances well calculated to make even the most submissive soldier oppose the authority that would have controlled him.

The light companies of fusileers, the forty-third and ninety-third regiments, and one hundred men from the West India regiment, led on by Colonel Rennie, succeeded in gaining possession of a redoubt on the bank of the river. Rennie had reached the works, and leaping on the wall, sword in hand, called upon his men to follow him; he had scarcely spoken when he fell by the fatal aim of a rifleman. Jackson, hearing that the redoubt was in possession of the enemy, sent a detachment instantly to retake it. Before its arrival, however, the enemy had abandoned it, and were retiring. They were severely galled by such of our guns as could be brought to bear. The levee afforded them considerable protection; yet, by Commodore Patterson's redoubt on the right bank, they suffered greatly. Enfiladed by this on their advance, they had been greatly annoyed, and now in their retreat were no less severely assailed. Numbers found a grave in the ditch before our line; and of those who gained the redoubt, not one it is believed escaped; they were shot down as fast as they entered. The route along which they had advanced and retired was strewed with bodies. Affrighted at the carnage, they moved from the scene hastily and in confusion. Our batteries were still continuing the slaughter, and cutting them down at every step; safety seemed only to be attainable when they should have retired without the range of our shot; which, to troops galled as severely as they were, was too remote a relief. Pressed by this consideration, they fled to the ditch, whither the right division had retreated, and there remained until night permitted them to retire.

Thus ended the battle of the 8th, one of the most glorious, as well as the most important in its results, that has ever been fought upon American soil.

The loss of the British in the main attack on the left bank has been at different times variously stated. The killed, wounded, and prisoners, ascertained on the next day after the battle by Colonel Hayne, the inspector-general, places it at 2600. General Lambert's report to Lord Bathurst makes it but 2070. From prisoners, however, and information and circumstances derived through other sources, it must have been even greater than is stated by either. Among them was the commander-in-chief, and Major-general Gibbs, who died of his wounds the next day, besides many of their most valuable and distinguished officers; while the loss of the Americans in killed and wounded was but thirteen. Our effective force at the line on the left bank was 3700, while that of the enemy was not less than 9000.

Never were officers more deceived than the British in the result of this battle. They had no belief that militia could withstand the attack of a regular army. One fact is told which confirms this. When repulsed from our line, they were fully persuaded

BATTLE OF NEW ORLEANS.

that the information given by the deserter, on the
night of the 6th, was false, and that, instead of
pointing out the ground defended by our militia, he
had shown them the place occupied by our best
troops. Enraged at what they believed an inten-
tional deception, they called their informant before
them to account for the mischief he had done. It
was in vain he urged his innocence, and, with the
most solemn protestations, declared he had stated
the fact truly as it was. They could not be convinced,—it was impossible that they had contended
against any but the best-disciplined troops; and,
without further ceremony, the poor fellow, suspended
in view of the camp, expiated on a tree, not his
crime, for what he had stated was true, but their
error in underrating an enemy who had already
afforded abundant evidences of valour. In all their
future trials with our countrymen, may they be no
less deceived, and discover in our yeomanry a determination to sustain with firmness a government
which knows nothing of oppression; but which, on
an enlarged and liberal scale, aims to secure the independence and happiness of man. If the people
of the United States,—free almost as the air they
breathe,—shall at any time omit to maintain their
privileges and their government, then, indeed, will

it be idle longer to speak of the rights of men, or of their capacity to govern themselves: the dream of liberty must fade away and perish for ever, no more to be remembered or thought of.

After the battle of the 8th of January, Jackson could have captured every man of the British force that was upon the land, if he had been supplied with arms, according to his own repeated urgent requests, and agreeably to the promises that were made him. Not having arms, he was compelled to let the remainder of the " heroes of the Peninsula" escape. The British embarked their remaining forces, and . sailed away from the shores which had witnessed their sanguinary defeat.   Enthusiastic rejoicings enlivened the city of New Orleans for many successive days.

CHAPTER XXI.

NEW ORLEANS AFTER THE BATTLE.

HOUGH the enemy had withdrawn from New Orleans in the manner which has been stated, Jackson could not be sure that they would not return. Against this contingency, he prepared himself by cautious arrangements in the distribution of his force and the construction of new defences at assailable points, before he returned to New Orleans. In that city he was received as a deliverer—every mind was kindled to enthusiasm from the consideration of the evils which he had averted, as well as of the victories which he had gained. The most solemn and lively demonstrations of public respect and gratitude succeeded each other daily, until the period of his departure for Nashville, soon after the annunciation of the peace concluded at Ghent, between Great Britain and the United States.

Though honoured and cherished by the larger part of the citizens of New Orleans, he was not without occasion to display the energy and decision of his character, in a way that favoured the ends of jealousy and detraction. Anonymous articles, calculated to excite mutiny among his troops, and afford the enemy dangerous intelligence, (for it must be recollected that the British commander did not take his final leave of Louisiana until the 18th, and was still in the neighbourhood,) appeared at this time, in one of the newspapers of New Orleans. Jackson caused the author of the articles to be revealed to him by the editor of the paper, when he found that the traitor was no less a personage than one of the members of the State Legislature. This, however, did not hinder Jackson from causing his immediate arrest and imprisonment. Application was made to one of the judges for a writ of *habeas corpus*, which was immediately granted and issued. We have already mentioned that Jackson arrested the judge. We now advert again to this incident, in order to relate what followed. The General had not yet raised the edict of martial law, (which he had been obliged to impose on the city upon undertaking its defence,) there being, as yet, no certain intelligence that the enemy had taken their de-

parture, and the news of the peace of Ghent not yet
having reached New Orleans. Within a few days,
the cessation of hostilities was announced officially.
The judge was restored to his post, and the exercise
of his functions. Without loss of time a rule of
court was granted for General Jackson to appear
and show cause why an attachment for contempt
should not issue, on the ground that he had refused
to obey a writ, and imprisoned the organ of the law
He did not hesitate to appear and submit a full and
very able answer, justifying his proceedings. After
argument before the court, the rule was made abso-
lute; an attachment sued out, and Jackson brought
up to answer interrogatories. He declined answer-
ing them, but asked for the sentence, which the
judge then proceeded to pass. It was *a fine of one
thousand dollars.* The spectators who crowded the
hall, betrayed the strongest indignation. As soon
as he entered his carriage, it was seized by the
people, and drawn by them to the coffee-house, amid
the acclamations of a large concourse. When he
arrived at his quarters, he put the amount of his fine
into the hands of his aid-de-camp, and caused it to
be discharged without delay. He was scarcely
beforehand with the citizens, who in a short time
raised the sum among themselves by contribution

and were anxious to be permitted to testify at once
their gratitude and shame. What was thus collected was appropriated at his request to a charita-
ble institution. He enjoyed the consciousness that
the powers which the exigency of the times forced
him to assume, had been exercised exclusively for
the public good, and that they had saved the country.
In 1821, the corporation of New Orleans voted *fifty
thousand dollars* for erecting a marble statue appropriate to his military services. The same body
gave also one thousand dollars for a portrait of him,
painted by Mr. Earle of Nashville. And the Congress of the United States, in the session of 1844–5,
thirty years after the injury was inflicted, made
ample and honourable restitution, by voting that the
amount of the fine, with interest in full, should be
reimbursed to General Jackson.

CHAPTER XXII.

SEMINOLE CAMPAIGN.

N the month of March, General Jackson returned once more to his home in Tennessee, carrying with him tne grateful regrets and kind regards of the people of Louisiana.

On his return to Nashville (a journey of eight hundred miles) he saw on every side marks of exultation and delight. It must be within the memory of most of our elder readers, what was the sensation produced throughout the union by the tidings from New Orleans, and what the popular enthusiasm concerning the merits of "Old Hickory."

For two years afterwards he remained on his farm, retaining his rank in the army; but chiefly occupied with rural pleasures and labours. In this interval the portion of the Seminoles who were driven into Florida, combining with fugitive negroes

K

from the adjoining states, and instigated by British adventurers, whose objects were blood and rapine, became formidable in numbers and hardihood, and began to execute schemes of robbery and vengeance against the Americans of the frontiers. It having been represented to the American government that murders had been committed on our defenceless citizens, General Gaines, the acting commander in the southern district, was ordered, in the summer of 1817, with a considerable force, to take a station near the borders for their protection. He was at first directed to keep within the territorial limits of the United States, and abstain from every attempt to cross the Florida line; but to demand of the Indians the perpetrators of the crimes thus committed, without involving the innocent, and without a general rupture with the deluded savages.

Murders having been ascertained to have been committed, attended with aggravating circumstances of rapine and cruelty, General Gaines made the demand, in conformity with his orders. The savages, however, deceived by the representations of certain foreign incendiaries and traders, who were among them, and who taught them to believe that they would receive assistance and encouragement from the British, not only refused to give up the murlerers, but repeated their massacres whenever an opportunity offered. While these things were going on, news reached the government that Lieutenant Scott, an officer acting under General Gaines, with forty-seven persons, men, women, and children, in a boat on the Apalachicola River, about two miles below the junction of the Flint and Chattahoochie, were surprised by an ambuscade of Indians, fired upon, and the whole detachment killed or captured, except six men, who contrived to escape by flight. Those who were taken alive were wantonly butchered after their capture by the ferocious savages, who seized the little children, and dashed their brains out against the side of the boat, murdering all the helpless females, except one, who was afterwards retaken.

The government, on the receipt of this news, saw at once the necessity of adopting energetic measures, and immediately issued orders to General Jackson to repair to Fort Scott, and take the command of the forces in that quarter, with authority in case he should deem it necessary, to call upon the executives of the adjoining states for additional troops. They also authorized him to cross the Florida line if necessary to the execution of his orders. Florida, it must be recollected, was still in possession of the Spaniards.

He was referred to the previous orders to General Gaines, and directed to concentrate his forces, and adopt " measures necessary to terminate a conflict which had been avoided from considerations of humanity, but which had now become indispensable from the settled hostility of the savage enemy." In January following, the Secretary of War, in a letter to General Gaines, said, " The honour of the United States requires that the war with the Seminoles should be terminated speedily, and with exemplary punishment for hostilities so unprovoked." Under these orders, and in this critical state of affairs, General Jackson, having first collected Tennessee volunteers, with that zeal and promptness which have ever marked his career, repaired to the post assigned, and assumed the command. The necessity of crossing the line into Florida was no longer a subject of doubt. A large force of Indians and negroes had made that territory their refuge, and the Spanish authority was either too weak or too indifferent to restrain them; and to comply with orders given him from the department of war, he penetrated immediately into the Seminole towns, driving the enemy before him, and reduced them to

ashes. In the council-house of the king of the Mick-
asukians, more than fifty fresh scalps, and in an
adjacent house, upwards of three hundred scalps, of
all ages and sexes, were found; and in the centre
of the public square a red pole was erected, crowned
with scalps, known by the hair to have belonged to
the companions of Lieutenant Scott.

To inflict merited punishment upon these barba-
rians, and to prevent a repetition of these massacres,
by bringing the war to a speedy and successful termination, he pursued his march to St. Marks: there
he found, conformably to previous information, that
the Indians and negroes had demanded the surrender
of the post to them; and that the Spanish garrison,
according to the commandant's own acknowledge-
ment, was too weak to support it. He ascertained
also that the enemy had been supplied with the
means of carrying on the war, from the commandant
of the post; that foreign incendiaries, instigating
the savages, had free communication with the fort:
councils of war were permitted by the commandant
.o be held by the chiefs and warriors within his own
quarters — the Spanish store-houses were appropriated to the use of the hostile party, and actually
filled with goods belonging to them, and property
known to have been plundered from American citi-

zens, was purchased from them by the commandant, while he professed friendship to the United States. General Jackson, therefore, did not hesitate to demand of the commandant of St. Marks, the surrender of that post that it might be garrisoned by an American force, and, when the Spanish officer hesitated, he entered the fort by force, though without bloodshed, the enemy having fled, and the garrison being too weak to make opposition. From this place he marched upon Suwaney, seized the stores of the enemy and burnt their villages.

A variety of circumstances now convinced General Jackson that the savages had commenced the war, and persisted in their barbarity. He also arrested at St. Marks several of the British incendiaries who had excited them to hostilities. One Alexander Arbuthnot, who was an Indian trader, was taken at St. Marks, where he had been living an inmate in the family of the commandant. He was tried by a court of enquiry of thirteen respectable officers, and sentenced to be hung, which sentence was immediately carried into execution.

Robert Ambrister, formerly a lieutenant in the British marine corps, was also tried; and it having been proved that he had not only encouraged and assisted the hostile savages, but had also led them, ne was sentenced by the court to receive fifty stripes, and to be confined, with a ball and chain, to hard labour for twelve calender months. General Jackson, however, disapproved of this sentence, which he did not think sufficiently severe, and the case being reconsidered, Ambrister was sentenced to be shot, which sentence was carried into execution forthwith.

Having thus far effected his objects, General Jackson considered the war at an end. St. Marks being garrisoned by an American force; the Indian towns of Mickasuky and Suwaney destroyed; the two Indian chiefs who had been the prime movers and leaders of the savages, one of whom commanded the party that murdered Lieutenant Scott and his companions, and the two principal foreign instigators, Arbuthnot and Ambrister, having been taken and executed, the American commander ordered the Georgia militia, who had joined him, to be discharged, and was about to return himself to Tennessee. But he soon learned that the Indians and negroes were collecting in bands west of the Appalachicola, which would render it necessary for him to send a detachment to scour the country in that quarter. While preparing for this object, he was informed that the Indians were admitted freely by

the governor of Pensacola ; that they were collecting
in large numbers, five hundred being in Pensacola
on the 15th of April, many of whom were known to
be hostile, and had just escaped from the pursuit of
our troops, that the enemy were furnished with
ammunition and supplies, and received intelligence
of the movements of our forces, from that place ;
that a number of them had sallied out and murdered
eighteen of our citizens, settlers upon the Alabama,
and were immediately received by the governor, and
by him transported across the bay, that they might
elude pursuit.

These facts being ascertained by General Jackson
from unquestionable authority, he immediately took
up his line of march towards Pensacola, at the head
of a detachment of about 1200 men, for the purpose
of counteracting the views of the enemy. On the
18th of May, he crossed the Appalachicola at the
Ocheese village, with the view of scouring the
country west of that river : and, on the 23d of the
same month, he received a communication from the
governor of West Florida, protesting against his
entrance into that province, commanding him to
retire from it, and declaring that he would repel
force by force, if he should not obey. This communication, together with other indications of hos-

tility in the governor, who had been well advised of the object of General Jackson's operations, determined the measures to be pursued. He marched directly to Pensacola, and took possession of that place the following day, the governor having fled to Fort Carlos de Barrancas; which post, after a feeble resistance, surrendered on the 28th. By these events, the Indians and fugitive negroes were deprived of all means of continuing their depredations, or screening themselves from the arm of justice.

There were, however, scattered and marauding parties; and, to prevent these from making inroads on the frontier settlers, Jackson ordered a couple of volunteer companies to scour the country between the Mobile and Appalachicola rivers.

Thus ended the campaign of the Seminole war, which, though not distinguished by any heavy battles, was, nevertheless, a most arduous and exhausting species of warfare.

CHAPTER XXIII.

JACKSON AFTER THE SEMINOLE CAMPAIGN.

JACKSON returned to Nashville, from the Seminole campaign, in June, 1818, and retired to his quiet Hermitage. New acknowledgements and new marks of admiration, poured in upon him from all sides. If the general government deemed it expedient to restore to the Spaniards the posts of St. Marks and Pensacola, they, nevertheless, applauded and defended what he had done. The British cabinet, moreover, approved of the treatment of Arbuthnot and Ambrister, who had acted contrary to the laws of nations and of humanity. The conduct of the Tennessee warrior was, however, destined to be most vehemently arraigned in another quarter,—in the House of Representatives; where a motion was made to condemn these acts of the Seminole war; the motion was, however, triumphantly rejected by a majority of the

House. A most eloquent orator proclaiming tha "he most cheerfully acquitted General Jackson of any intention to violate the laws of his country or the obligations of humanity." Whoever studies Jackson's ample despatches in the campaign, and the speeches delivered in his behalf, must be convinced that he did neither, and that in making an example of the two instigators and confederates of the savages, and seizing upon fortresses which were only used for hostile purposes, he avenged and served the cause of humanity, and the highest national interests.

His desire of explaining his transactions in person, to the government, and defending himself on every side, carried him to Washington at this period. Thence he came to Philadelphia, and proceeded to New York. Wherever he appeared, crowds attended with unceasing plaudits. In each of these cities public dinners and balls were given in his honour; military escorts provided; addresses delivered by deputations; and to these his answers were uniformly pertinent and dignified. At New York, on the 19th of February, he received the freedom of the city in a gold box; and there, as well as in Baltimore, the municipal councils requested and obtained his portrait, to be placed in their halls.

While he was on this excursion, a report, connected with the history of the Seminole war, and extremely hostile to his character, was made from a committee of the Senate of the United States. It had not the concurrence of the ablest members of the committee, and it was brought forward at too late a period of the session of Congress to be discussed. Nothing more was supposed to be meant by its author than to cast an indictment before the public. It was repelled triumphantly, in a defence which was published in the National Intelligencer, on the 5th of March, and which has been ascribed to General Jackson. He felt deeply imputations which he knew to be not only false, but utterly irreconcilable with his nature. The issue of all the reports and harangues was such as might give additional comfort to his domestic hours on his return to his farm, where he enjoyed again a period of repose.

CHAPTER XXIV.

JACKSON AS GOVERNOR OF FLORIDA.

WHEN the treaty with Spain, ceding the Floridas, was finally ratified, Congress passed a law empowering the President to vest in such person or persons as he might select, all the military, civil, and judicial authority exercised by the officers of the Spanish government. The President, under this law, appointed General Jackson, to act in the first place as commissioner for receiving the provinces, and then to assume the government of them. It was intended and expressed that the American governor should exercise all the functions belonging to the Spanish governors, Captain-General and Intendants, until Congress should provide a system of administration as in the instances of the other territories.

The selection of Jackson was not a mere mark of honour or testimonial of public gratitude. His intimate acquaintance with the country, and the energy of his nature, recommended him specially for the post of governor.   Florida was overrun with desperadoes of every description; it was the resort of a motley horde of smugglers, negro dealers, and adventurers of all kinds and nations, and had become the theatre of misrule and mischief.   The reputation of Jackson was calculated to overawe this mass of villainy.

It was not without reluctance that General Jackson entered upon this arduous office, but a sense of duty compelled him to accept the office, and he accordingly repaired to the scene of his labours.

On the first of July, 1821, he issued at Pensacola his proclamation, announcing that possession had been taken of the territory, and the authority of the United States established.

He at once adopted vigorous measures for producing a proper administration.   Courts were organized and a police was instituted.

It was not long until a case came before Jackson, requiring the exertion of his official power with firmness and decision.

By the treaty with Spain, all documents relating to property or sovereignty were required to be delivered up to the American authorities.   Some of these had already been submitted to General Jackson, in his capacity of governor; but, upon the 22d of August, he received a petition from certain individuals, stating that some deeds, relating to property, had been feloniously retained by the Spanish ex-governor, Callava, and that they were then in the hands of a man called Sousa. Jackson immediately ordered three officers to wait upon Sousa, and demand the documents. Sousa exhibited them to the officers, but refused to give them up, as they had been intrusted to him by Callava. Jackson ordered Sousa to appear before him, who returned answer that the papers had been sent to the house of the ex-governor Callava. Two officers were then sent by Jackson to the house of Callava, with orders to demand the papers, and, in case they were refused, to require both Callava and his steward, who had received them from Sousa, to appear before the governor. The Spaniard insisted at first upon retaining the papers, and, after promising to surrender them, when a list was furnished, and failing to do so, and obstinately refusing to obey the summons in any manner, he was finally conducted under guard to the office of the governor. When there, he was informed of the nature and propriety of the demand made upon him, and apprized that the further with holding of the papers would be regarded as a contempt of the governor's judicial authority, and subject him to imprisonment. He would do nothing but dictate protests, when the patience of Jackson being exhausted, he, his steward, and Sousa were committed to prison, until the papers should be obtained.

The next morning, the box in which the papers had been seen, was seized and opened by officers specially commissioned. It had been carefully sealed by Callava, and was found to contain what was sought. Callava and his companions were then released from jail. The records thus recovered related to the estate of a person who died at Pensacola, about the year 1807, having made his will, and bequeathed his property to several orphan females, who had never received any portion of it, owing to the dishonesty of the individuals who were at the same time its depositaries and debtors. Callava himself had made decrees in favour of the heirs, which were discovered in the box and had been suppressed under corrupt influence. It was the object of Callava to carry off all the evidence necessary for redress. He afterwards published in the American papers an exposition of the treatment he had received, and was convicted of misrepresenta-

tion, by the counter statements of gentlemen in
Pensacola. To have allowed the wrong which was
designed to be committed, would have been a
disgrace to the dignity and justice of the government of the United States, as well as to humanity.
The just language of Jackson in his justification of
the affair to the President was: "When men of
high standing attempt to trample on the rights of
the weak, they are the fittest objects for example or
punishment. In general, the great can protect themselves, but the poor and humble require the arm and
shield of the law."

Among the civil officers sent to Florida on its
occupation by our government, was a former Senator of the United States, Elegius Fromentin, who
went in the capacity of a judge, with a jurisdiction
limited to cases that might arise under the revenue
laws, and the acts of Congress prohibiting the intro-
duction of slaves. This gentleman consented, at
the instigation of some of the friends of Callava,
to issue a writ of *habeas corpus* to extricate the
Spaniard from confinement. The general Judiciary
Act for the United States, under which alone the
judge could claim the right of thus interfering, had
not been extended to the Floridas. Jackson displayed his characteristic decision and intelligence

in this case, by citing Fromentin to appear before
him and answer to the charge of a contempt of the
superior court, and a serious misdemeanor. The
prisoner was released, the papers having been obtained before Mr. Fromentin was able to present
himself, pursuant to the summons. The General
was then content with defining to him the limits of
his competency as judge, and uttering a severe re-
proof of his precipitation. Very bitter complaints
were afterwards made by both parties to the execu-
tive at Washington.

This, even, was not the end of the Callava case,
as it has been called. Several Spanish officers who
had remained with the ex-governor in the province
ventured to publish, in a Pensacola paper, an article
with their signatures, in which they accused the
General of violence and tyranny. It was stipulated
in the treaty of cession, that all the Spanish officers
should be withdrawn from the territories ceded,
within six months after the ratification of the treaty.
More than this term had elapsed. Jackson issued
his proclamation without delay, commanding them,
as trespassers and disturbers of the public peace, to
depart in the course of a week. They had not the
folly to remain. About the same period, many
mportant documents which the Spaniards had

no right to retain, were attempted to be withheld by the ex-governor of East Florida. Jackson, on hearing of this attempt, transmitted, by mail, his orders to take forcible possession of them; which was done accordingly. The ex-governor protested; but upon insufficient grounds, and with personal disgrace.

These occurrences produced much discussion in the newspapers, and violent remonstrances from the Spanish minister, but the acts of General Jackson were fully justified as soon as the facts became generally known.

On the 7th of October, Jackson delegated his power to two gentlemen, his secretaries, and returned to Nashville. In his valedictory address to the citizens of Florida, he informed them that he had completed the temporary organization of the two provinces. He stated and justified his acts in the case of Callava.

The injuries which his health had suffered, forbade him to protract his residence in Florida.

Before his departure, he received from the citizens spontaneous public manifestations of esteem and gratitude. Attempts were made at the ensuing session of Congress, to obtain a condemnation of his conduct towards Callava, but they utterly failed, both with the Legislature and the people. On the 4th of July, 1822, the governor of Tennessee, by order of the Legislature, presented him with a sword as a testimonial "of the high respect" entertained by the state for his public services. And, on the 20th of August, of the same year, the members of the General Assembly of Tennessee recommended him to the union for the office of President—a recommendation which was repeated by the Legislature of Alabama, and various assemblages of private citizens in other parts of the country. In the autumn of 1823, he was elected to the Senate of the United States; social honours were heaped upon him at Washington, and he was every day receiving evidences of the high respect entertained for him on all sides.

Before his election to the Senate, he was appointed Minister Plenipotentiary to the government of Mexico, but he declined the office, in consequence of his repugnance to the monarchical system of government which then existed in that country.

CHAPTER XXV.

JACKSON BECOMES PRESIDENT OF THE UNITED STATES.

N 1824, when a new President was to be chosen, Jackson was put in nomination as a candidate for the office; but though he had more votes than any other candidate, yet he was not elected. The reader will ask how this can be? it is thus: The law is, that *electors* of the President shall be chosen by the people in every state; that these electors shall each give their votes for some one person to be President; that any candidate who has a majority of the votes of the whole of the electors shall be the President; but, if there be no one who has a majority of the whole of the votes of the electors, then the President shall be chosen by the members of the House of Representatives; but that there they shall vote by *states ;* and that each state shall have *one vote, and no more.* Now, there were

four candidates having votes of electors, as follows :—

Jackson.................................... 99
Adams 84
Crawford 47
Clay 31
                                    ——
                            Total, 261

Therefore, Jackson not having a majority of the
whole, the other kind of election took place; and as
they were the large states which were for him, and
the small states which were for Adams, the election
by the House of Representatives made Adams
President, with a minority of the votes of the people.

Adams's four years having expired, he was once
more a candidate; but the field was now clear of
Clay and of Crawford, and the votes of the electors
stood thus:

Jackson 178
Adams 83
                                    ——
                            Total, 261

Jackson was, therefore, in 1828, elected President
of the United States, and his first term of office
having expired, he was, in 1832, re-elected by a
triumphant majority over his opponent, Henry Clay

It need hardly be observed that General Jackson,
during his political life, as every great man must
made a large number of enemies. The greater part

of these enemies grew out of General Jackson's opposition to the Bank of the United States.

The many and strong prejudices engendered by his bold and energetic administration of public affairs, will gradually become less as time erases from memories the influence of his policy upon individual interests and happiness. There will always, however, be a diversity of opinions among the most intelligent and honest, as to the effects of his remarkable career upon the character and prosperity of the country.

General Jackson, upon retiring from the Presidential chair, in 1836, returned to his quiet home at the Hermitage, near Nashville, Tennessee, whence his influence was silently exerted upon our politics for the residue of his life. He continued, till the end, to be recognised as the chief of the great party over which he had so long presided, and was consulted almost as an oracle upon all important questions.

CHAPTER XXVI.

THE LAST HOURS OF JACKSON.

E come now to the last scene in the life of the great soldier and statesman, and shall dwell with particularity upon the incidents of his death. He died at his home in Tennessee, on the afternoon of the 8th day of June, 1845. Mr. William Tyack, of New York, has published an account of his visit to the Hermitage, which he left the Wednesday before the ex-president expired, and from his journal we take the following paragraphs:

"*Wednesday, May* 28.—On my arrival, I found General Jackson more comfortable than he had been, although his disease is not abated, and his long and useful life is rapidly drawing to its close. He has not been in a condition to lie down during the last four months. His feet and legs, his hands and arms, are very much swollen with dropsy, which has invaded his whole system. Bandages are drawn tight around the parts most affected, to prevent, as much as possible, the increase of water. He has scarcely any use of his hands. The bandages are removed several times in the twenty-four hours, and the parts rubbed severely to restore animation and the circulation of the blood. He has not strength to stand; his respiration is very short, and attended with much difficulty, and the whole progress of his disease is accompanied with great suffering. He has no sleep except by opiates.

"*Thursday, May* 29.—General Jackson is rather more comfortable, having obtained some sleep through medicines. This day he sat a while to Mr. Healy, who had been sent by Louis Philippe, to paint his portrait. Mr. Healy told me that it was the design of the King of the French to place Jackson's by the side of Washington's, which already hangs in his gallery—the most celebrated and interesting historical collection in the world—and to surround them with the pictures of the most eminent of American generals and statesmen. Mr. Healy is commissioned by the king to paint the portraits of some twelve of our most distinguished patriots, to accompany those of Washington and Jackson—the greatest and best men our country has produced—as well as some of the most prom-inent politicians of the present time. Messrs. John Quincy Adams and Henry Clay were named by Mr. Healy to me. He was enabled to make much pro-gress in his work to-day, and, as usual, the General received many visiters—more than thirty. All were admitted, from the humblest to the most renowned, to take the venerable chieftain by the hand and bid him farewell. Among them was General Jessup, an old friend and companion in arms. The meeting of these most faithful and gallant soldiers and servants of the republic was deeply interesting and affecting. A reverend gentleman called to inquire in regard to the General's health, his faith, and religious hope. He said, " Sir, I am in the hands of a merciful God. I have full confidence in his goodness and mercy. My lamp of life is nearly out, and the last glimmer is come. I am ready to depart when called. The Bible is true. The principles and statutes of that holy book have been the rule of my life, and I have tried to conform to its spirit as near as possible Upon that sacred volume I rest my hope of eternal salvation, through the merits and blood of our blessed Lord and Saviour, Jesus Christ." Nothing farther was said upon the subject.

"*Friday, May* 30.—The General passed a bad

JACKSON AT THE HERMITAGE.

night; no sleep—extremely feeble this morning. Mr
Healy, with considerable exertions on the part of
the General, was enabled to finish the portrait. on
which he laboured with great care. It was presented
to the General. After examining it for some minutes, he remarked to Mr. Healy, "I am satisfied,
sir, that you stand at the head of your profession;
if I may be allowed to judge of my own likeness, I
can safely concur in the opinion of my family, that it
is the best that has been taken. I feel very much
obliged to you, sir, for the very great labour and
care you have been pleased to bestow upon it."
The family were all highly gratified with its faithful-
ness. I consider it the most perfect representation
I have ever seen, giving rather the remains of the
heroic personage, than the full life that made him
the most extraordinary combination of spirit and
energy, with a slender frame, the world ever saw.
At nine o'clock, as was the custom, all the General's
family—except the few who take their turn to watch
by his side—took their leave of him. Each of them
approached him, received his blessing, bade him
farewell, and kissed him, as it would seem, an eternal good-night—for he would say, "My work is done
for life." After his family retires, it is touching to
see this heroic man, who has faced every danger

with unyielding front, offer up his prayers for those
whom Providence has committed to his care; that
Heaven would protect and prosper them when he is
no more—praying still more fervently to God for
the preservation of his country, of the union, and
the people of the United States, from all foreign influence and invasion—tendering his forgiveness to
his enemies, and his gratitude to God for his support
and success through a long life, and for the hope of
eternal salvation, through the merits of our blessed
Redeemer. He exerts himself to discharge every
duty, and with all the anxious care that is possible;
but his debility and the unremitting anguish he
suffers have almost extinguished every power except
that of his intellect. Occasionally his distress pro-
duces spasmodic affections; yet, in the midst of the
worst paroxysms of pain, not a murmur, not even a
groan, escapes his lips. Great and just in life, calm
and resigned in death.

"*Saturday, May* 31.—The General passed a night
of distress, no sleep; extreme debility this morning,
attended with increased swelling of the abdomen
and all his limbs, and difficulty of breathing. He
said, "I hope God will grant me patience to submit to His holy will; He does all things well, and
blessed be His holy and merciful name." His Bible

is always near him; if he is in his chair, it is on the table by his side; when propped up in bed that sacred volume is laid by him, and he often reads it. He has no strength, and is lifted in and out of his sitting posture in bed to the same position in his chair. Nothing can exceed the affectionate care, vigilance, and never-ceasing efforts of his pious and devoted family, to administer to his relief; and yet, in the midst of the affliction which calls for so much attention and sympathy, kindness and hospitality to strangers are not omitted.

"*Sunday, June* 1.—"This day," the General said, "is the holy Sabbath, ordained by God, and set apart to be devoted to his worship and praise. I always attended service at church when I could; but now I can go no more." He desired the family to go, as many as could, and charged them to continue the education of the poor at the Sunday school. This new system of instruction, he said, which blended the duties of religion with those of humanity, he considered of vast importance; and spoke with an emphasis which showed his anxiety to impress it on the family. Mrs. Jackson, and her sister, Mrs. Adams, regularly attended to the teaching of the poor on the Sabbath. A part of the family went to church. The General looked out of the

window, and said, " This is apparently the last Sabbath I shall be with you; God's will be done—He
is kind and merciful." His look is often fixed with
peculiar affection on his grand-daughter Rachel,
named after his wife, whose memory he has so tenderly cherished. She has all the lovely and amiable
qualities for which the elder Mrs. Jackson was so
remarkable.

"*Monday, June 2.*—The General passed a restless
night—no sleep—an evident increase of the effects
of the disease. He read many letters, as usual.
Some of them were from persons of whom he had
no knowledge, asking for autographs, and making
other requests. The letters were opened by some
of the family. Mrs. Jackson or Mrs. Adams was
almost constantly with him. He looked over them;
those of importance were opened and read. Among
them was one from Major Donelson, charge d'af-
faires to Texas, giving an account of the almost in-
credible proceedings of the British agent, Elliot, to
prevent the annexation of Texas to the United
States. The General said, " We have made a disgraceful sacrifice of our territory; an important
portion of our country was given away to England
without a shadow of title on the part of the claim-
ants, as has been shown by the admissions of the

English ministers on referring, in Parliament, to the King's map, on which the true boundaries were delineated, and of which they were apprised when urging their demands. "Right on the side of the American people, and firmness in maintaining it," he continued, "with trust in God alone, will secure to them the integrity of the possessions of which the British government would now deprive them. I am satisfied that they will assert and vindicate what justice awards them; and that no part of our territory or country will ever be submitted to any arbitration but of the cannon's mouth." He felt grateful to a merciful Providence that had always sustained him through all his struggles, in the defence and for the independence and prosperity of his beloved country, and that he could give up his stewardship and resign his breath to the God who gave it, with the cheering reflection that the country was now settled down upon a firm, democratic basis; that the rights of the labouring classes were respected and protected, (for, he adds, it is from them that the country derives all its prosperity and greatness,) and to them we must ever look for defence of our soil when invaded. They have never refused. No, sir: and never will. Give them an honest government, freedom from monopolies and privileged classes, and hard money—not paper currency—for their hard labour, and all will be well. At two o'clock, P. M., his distress became suddenly very great. An express was sent to Nashville, twelve miles, for surgical aid. An operation was performed by Doctor Esleman, which produced great relief, although extreme prostration.

"*Tuesday, June* 3.—Much distress through the night. Opiates were freely administered, but sleep appeared to have passed from him. Calm, and perfectly resigned to the will of his Redeemer, he prayed to God to sustain him in this his hour of dissolution. At ten o'clock, A. M., Doctors Robinson and Walters arrived from Nashville, Doctor Esleman having remained with the General through the night. A consultation was held, and all that had been done was approved; all that could be done was to administer to the General's temporary wants. At four o'clock, P. M., I left his house for home. He expressed great solicitude in my behalf, but I was silent; the scene was too affecting; and I left this aged *soldier, statesman, and Christian patriot* with all the pious and hospitable inmates of the Hermitage, without the power of saying farewell."

We continue the narrative, from the declarations of Dr. Esleman, the attending physician:

Early in the morning, (Sunday,) he became con scious that the spark of life was nearly extinguished ; and, expecting to die before another sun would set, he sent for his family and domestics to receive his dying benediction. His remarks were full of affection and Christian resignation. His mind retained its vigour to the last, and his dying moments, even more than his early years, exhibited its highest intellectual light.

To his family and friends he said:—" Do not grieve that I am about to leave you, for I shall be better off. Although I am afflicted with pain and bodily suffering, these are as nothing compared with the sufferings of the Saviour of the world, who was put to death on the accursed tree. I have fulfilled my destiny on the earth, and it is better that this worn-out frame should go to rest, and my spirit take up its abode with the Redeemer."

He continued thus to address his relatives and friends at intervals, during the forenoon, and as, Dr. Esleman remarked, his confidence and faith in the great truths of religion seemed to be more firm and unwavering than any man he had ever seen die. He expressed a desire that Dr. Edgar of the Presby- terian Church, to which he himself belonged, should preach his funeral sermon, and that no pomp or parade should be made over his grave.

M

CHAPTER XXVII.

FUNERAL HONOURS—CHARACTER—PERSONAL APPEARANCE.

HE intelligence of General Jackson's death caused everywhere a profound sensation. In all the large cities, funeral honours were paid to his memory, and eulogiums were pronounced by the most eminent citizens. We close this memoir with the words of one of the most distinguished of our statesmen, and the ablest of those who opposed General Jackson's administration—Daniel Webster, who spoke as follows, before the Historical Society of New York:

"The character of General Jackson, while he lived, was presented in two relations to his country. He was a soldier and had commanded the armies of the Republic, and he has filled the office of Chief Magistrate. So far as regards his military reputation and merits, I partake fully in the general estimate. He was a soldier of dauntless courage, vigour and perseverance, an officer of skill and sagacity, of quickness of perception, and of prompt and resolute execution of his purposes. There is probably no division, at home or abroad, as to his merits in these particulars.

" During the whole of his civil administration, it happened that I was a member of the Senate of the United States; and it was my misfortune to be obliged to differ with him in regard to most of his leading measures. To me this was painful, because it much better suits my temper and feelings to be able to support the measures of government, than to find myself called upon by duty to oppose them.

" There were occasions, however, in the course of his administration, in which no duty of opposition devolved upon me. Some of these were not unimportant. There were times which appeared to me to be critical, calling for wisdom and energy on the part of the government, and in which measures proposed, and opinions expressed by him, seemed to me to be highly suitable to the exigency. On these occasions, I supported those measures with the same sincerity and zeal as if I had never differed from him before, or never expected to differ from him again.

" There is no doubt that he sought to distinguish

himself by exalting the character and honour of his country. And the occasion on which it was uttered rendered somewhat remarkable his celebrated senti- ment in favour of the preservation of the union. I believe he felt the sentiment with the utmost sin- cerity, and this cannot be denied to be one strong proof of his devotion to the true interests of his country.

"He has now ceased from his earthly labours; and affects the public interests of the State only by his example and the influence of his opinions. We may well suppose that in the last days and hours, and moments of his life, and with the full conscious- ness of the change then before him and so near, one of his warmest wishes would be, that whatever errors he might have committed should be passing and transitory in their effect upon the constitution and institutions of his country. And while we may well ascribe this praiseworthy and benign dying sentiment to him, let us, with equal ingenuousness, cherish the feeling that whatever he has accom- plished for the real good of the country, its true character and real glory, may remain a just inher- itance attached to his memory."

In the various critical situations in which he was placed by emergencies and the unlimited discretion cast upon him, he appears to have been governed by general and solid principles which he knew how to apply satisfactorily in explaining his measures. The very salutary energy and decision with which he pursued the course that he had deliberately concluded to be right and necessary, subjected him to the belief or charge of having acted merely from a vehement, overbearing, or arbitrary disposition. If his feelings were strongly roused and displayed against the timid or the traitorous portion of the inhabitants of New Orleans, who would have given the enemy an easy and fatal triumph—against the Spanish authorities in Florida who served the British and supplied the Seminoles—against Arbuthnot and Ambrister, the unwearied instigators and insidious confederates of the savages thirsting for American blood — against the impostor prophets, who had directed the butchery of white women and children, and whose occupation it was to incite depredation and murder—against a Spanish governor who would have violated a treaty and despoiled orphan females of their inheritance—we may say that both the warmth of those feelings, and the rigour with which they were manifested, will be easily excused by generous minds.

General Jackson was artificial in nothing. In

regard to business, he was indefatigable and saga
cious, and, in the course of his practice as a lawyer
he accumulated a competent estate.

In person, General Jackson was tall, and remark-
ably erect and thin. His weight bore no proportion
to his height, and his frame, in general, did not
appear fitted for trials such as it had borne. His
features were large; his eyes dark blue, with a keen
and strong glance; his eye-brows arched and prom-
inent, and his complexion that of the war-worn
soldier. His demeanour was easy and gentle: in
every station he was open and accessible to all.
The irritability of his temper, which was not denied
by his friends, produced contrasts in his manner and
countenance leading to very different conceptions
and representations as to both : but those who have
lived and acted with him bear unanimous testimony
to the general mildness of his carriage and the
kindness of his disposition. It is certain that he
inspired his soldiers, his military household, his
domestic circle, and his neighbours, with the most
affectionate sentiments. The impetuosity of nis
nature, his impatience of wrong and encroachment,
his contempt for meanness. and his tenaciousness
of just authority, involved him in bitter alter-
cations and sanguinary quarrels:—his resentments

were fiercely executed, and his censures rashly
uttered; yet he cannot be accused of wanton or
malicious violence; the sallies which may be deemed
intemperate can be traced to strong provocation,
operating, in most instances, upon his patriotic zeal
and the very generosity and loftiness of his spirit.

His amusements consisted chiefly in the manage-
ment of his domestic concerns, the sports of the turf,
and social intercourse. He was temperate in his
diet, and in all respects enjoyed a good private reputation.

> How sleep the brave, who sink to rest,
> By all their country's wishes blest !
> When Spring, with dewy fingers cold,
> Returns to seek their hallow'd mould,
> She there shall dress a sweeter sod,
> Than Fancy's feet have ever trod !
> By fairy forms their dirge is sung—
> By hands unseen their knell is rung—
> There Honour comes, a pilgrim grey,
> To bless the turf that wraps their clay —
> And Freedom shall awhile repair
> To dwell a weeping hermit there!

THE END.

www.ingramcontent.com/pod-product-compliance
Lightning Source LLC
Chambersburg PA
CBHW030547040726

47497CB00008B/2608